Ammar Abou-Rahma is a passionate and creative writer whose love for storytelling is evident in his work. With a background in information technology and a keen interest in literature, Ammar seamlessly weaves together the realms of creativity and innovation. Whether delving into the intricacies of fiction or exploring the latest developments in the digital world, Ammar brings a unique perspective and a gift for engaging narrative. His commitment to lifelong learning and curiosity have driven him to explore various subjects, making his writing both insightful and approachable.

When not immersed in the world of words, Ammar enjoys hiking, board games, and experimenting with new designs on his 3D printer. *The Upper Levels* is more than just a story for Ammar—it's an invitation to join him on a journey through the fascinating landscapes of imagination and discovery.

Ammar Abou-Rahma

THE UPPER LEVELS

AUSTIN MACAULEY PUBLISHERS™
LONDON • CAMBRIDGE • NEW YORK • SHARJAH

Copyright © Ammar Abou-Rahma 2024

The right of Ammar Abou-Rahma to be identified as the author of this work has been asserted by the author in accordance with Federal Law No. (7) of UAE, Year 2002, Concerning Copyrights and Neighboring Rights.

All rights reserved. No part of this publication may be reproduced, stored in a retrieval system, or transmitted in any form or by any means, electronic, mechanical, photocopying, recording, or otherwise, without the prior permission of the publishers.

Any person who commits any unauthorized act in relation to this publication may be liable to legal prosecution and civil claims for damages.

The age group that matches the content of the books has been classified according to the age classification system issued by the Ministry of Culture and Youth.

ISBN – 9789948753469– (Paperback)
ISBN – 9789948753476– (E-Book)

Application Number: MC-10-01-1126137
Age Classification: 17+

Printer Name: Print Global Ltd
Printer Address: Witchford, England

First Published 2024
AUSTIN MACAULEY PUBLISHERS FZE
Sharjah Publishing City
P.O Box [519201]
Sharjah, UAE
www.austinmacauley.ae
+971 655 95 202

In loving memory of my father:

To the man who kindled the flames of ambition within my heart, who nurtured my imagination, and who instilled in me the courage to pursue my passions—this book is a tribute to the indelible mark you've left on my soul. Your spirit lives on in every word, every page, and every achievement. Thank you for being my greatest inspiration and my forever hero.

I extend my heartfelt gratitude to my publishers, whose unwavering support and belief in this project have been instrumental in bringing my novel to life.

To my loving wife, your persistence and unwavering encouragement have been the driving force behind the realization of this dream. Your belief in my abilities, even during moments of self-doubt, has been a constant source of inspiration. Thank you for being my pillar of strength and for pushing me to share this story with the world.

To my daughter, your infectious enthusiasm and boundless curiosity have added an extra layer of joy to the journey of creating this novel. Your presence and the sparkle in your eyes have fueled my determination to create something meaningful for you and generations to come.

To a few of my friends who contributed, each in their own way, thank you for being a part of this journey. Your support has made this novel richer, and I am fortunate to have such a wonderful circle of friends who believe in the power of storytelling.

Together, you have been the foundation upon which this literary endeavor stands. This book is as much yours as it is mine, and I am profoundly grateful for the support and love that have surrounded its creation.

Chapter 1

I once heard that cockroaches will one day inherit the Earth, or at least outlive humans—supposedly. But how we all live isn't too dissimilar from a cockroach—surviving day by day with whatever food we can get our hands on. Perspective is a very delicate concept, even more so if your mindset is narrow. Simultaneously, reality and perspective could both be the same and yet the exact opposite. The lines are blurred for humanity, struggling to survive beneath the Earth, while the cockroaches proliferate and grow above.

Perhaps we're lucky to even be still alive in the year 2124—it's up to you to decide if your reality is your truth or not. The only thing I know for certain is that in one month, my whole reality will change. Turning eighteen has always been a significant milestone for people from diverse backgrounds and generations. Ever since it was the age at which you graduated high school, the military draft age, and the age your brain develops to a mature age. This includes physical, emotional, social, and cognitive development. Lucky for us, we have all the preserved books and Wikipedia—the only source of information that has survived this apocalypse.

By focusing on the details of individuals' lives in those novels, you learn a lot about the previous generations that lived outside. I often wonder if I will ever experience the same life as in books. I don't complain, though. I have a loving and caring family and am rarely ever short on food. What more can I ask for? In all fairness, they're not really my family, but if a stranger has cared for and raised you all your life, wouldn't you call them family as well?

I don't remember my actual family very well. Apparently, we became separated at a really young age. At least that's what Odin keeps telling me. Odin is like a mystical creature who knows all but would only feed you knowledge sparingly. Somehow, I think he is just merciful. Who knows what he knows? His knowledge could be too much for one person to handle.

"Since you're not studying, come here. You can help me out, but you better hope your exam does not test your cognitive skills. Otherwise, you'll be staying here with me. I would like that very much," Odin says with a laugh.

Odin pulls me closer to him with his massive arms. He is huge, his arms engulfing my whole neck and the bottom part of the back of my head. He is like a teddy bear until he's angry, I imagine. Though I have never ever seen him angry, I would definitely not want to flip that coin.

I let out a slow exhale. I need to finish up my tasks, so I can review them one last time for that exam. The exam will literally change my life, assuming all goes as planned with the final scores. Very few people manage to pass and ameliorate their way of life to a higher status. I know because I hear it from everyone around me who seems intent on reminding me that there is no way up from here.

I have lived in this bunker all my life, but I have always wanted to move to the upper levels ever since I could talk because I'm confident that's where my father is. Odin doesn't tell me much about my family or what happened, but I know that my father was a great scientist who wanted to change the world. He left a shadow behind, one that follows me everywhere, constantly whispering in my ear that I can be more than this.

I wish I could remember how he looks like at least. All I can remember is he has my same hazel eyes and a short beard that I haven't gotten to yet. One day, I will see him, and I'll tell him all about my current family and all the cool concept ideas I have that we could work on.

One day soon.

"Odin, I finished all my tasks for today and finished studying. Can I go with Sabrina and hang out by the river?"

"Go ahead, son, but do not stay for too long!"

Sabrina is Odin's daughter, and she's the closest thing I have to a sister and best friend. We have lived most of our lives together, and we will be both taking our exams together next month. She's so smart, but her specialty is her connection with nature and medicine. It's like she has a green thumb but for people. She can heal anyone and cares for everyone equally, and admittedly, that's what I love most about her.

On the other hand, my specialty is my knowledge of technology. My only complaint is that I am so limited with the resources I have here on this level. We are not as privileged as the upper levels. They get to have all the best resources in general, and we get the scraps here. That is why this is the most crucial exam in everyone's life. We all wish to move up and have a better life.

Sabrina walks toward me from the back and taps my right shoulder and keeps walking ahead from my left side. I look behind me to my right side, realizing she's already ahead of me and ready to head out.

This silly joke of hers never gets old.

Her green eyes twinkle a bit. "I wonder if you will ever learn to look at me from the first tap. Now come on, let's go before it gets late." She smirks at me in her yet another successful jest.

"Coming, coming! Just gonna grab some snacks."

I grab some homemade cheese bites and some crackers and head out with Sabrina. She walks, but her feet almost prance, floating between each step. There's such a gracefulness about her that it often leaves my words tangled up in my mouth. And though her long brown hair is generally tied up in a tail or delicate bun, sometimes I catch her with it down. It frames her face so beautifully.

"Keep up," she urges with a wave of her hand.

I nod and dash forward. There are two main levels in the bunker, but each level has subdivisions. Most of our agricultural needs are sustained at a specific level further underground. The river is not too far from home, but it's one of my favorite spots since it's one of the spots that feel chilly compared to the rest of our lower level. The lower the bunker, the hotter it generally gets since we are closer to the Earth's core. Still, since we have managed to get agriculture in our bunkers, we also managed to control the temperature to a certain extent.

Sabrina rushes directly to our favorite hangout spot. It is a small boulder near the river, just enough for two people to sit on and relax. We sit down on the rock. It's my favorite feeling since it's slightly cold to the touch.

"So what have you brought us today, mister? Wait, let me guess. I will bet you an extra portion of cheese and crackers that that's what you got. So am I right?"

She always knows everything somehow, and I have no idea how she does it. So I grab the snacks and place them down as we munch down on them and chat.

"So what's your plans once you get up there?" I say as I take another bite of my mini cheese cracker sandwich.

"Honestly, I haven't decided yet if I even want to go. I am really happy here with family and friends. Plus, there are a lot of people in need of help. I can't just leave them and go up just like that. I heard people who go up never come down." She tugs at her monotone shirt for a moment, toying with the fabric while giving it deeper thought.

I look down. Now that she's mentioned it, it's true. I have never seen anyone come back down to the lower levels. You might hear stories about them but never actually see them.

"Well, I'd like to change that then. I will go up there and keep going back and forth. After all, how could I forget about you and Odin? I will find a way to get you guys out of there too."

The corners of her mouth pull into a smile. "Sounds like more of a reason for me to stay since you will be passing by anyway. No, but really, people here are in need, and if all the fortunate people keep moving upward, then we won't have anyone left here to help around those who need it the most."

Her eyes move down to her lap, where she toys with her fingers between bites. "This is what my mother did, why shouldn't I? Plus, I will have you as my inside connection.

We would hook each other up with whatever resources we can!"

"Well, you do make some good points there, so you win for now. I won't give up on you, though," I say as I try to smile through the painful truth she has spilled on me.

I hate and love how she is always right. For now, all I can do is do my best and keep moving forward with my plan. I wish for change in this world of ours. We can't stay living limited and restricted forever like this. There must be more than just this bunker we all live in. On top of that, limited to these hierarchy levels.

Our chatter quiets down a bit later, and I start admiring the world we, as a community, have created. I have been here so many times and lived my whole life in this bunker, but it still always amazes me how far we have reached to create this world of ours. From the grass surrounding most of this level to the different livestock slurping from the river stream across the land, to even the biomass used to fertilize our plantations.

Even when the world was about to end, even though it was kind of our fault, we still managed to put our issues aside for a moment and work together. As I stare across the river that divides the livestock and the plants, a thought hits me.

I take a deep earthy breath and change the topic. "Okay, here is another question. I know we don't really know much about the outside world aside from that big nuclear war that destroyed any potential for a normal life outside. But if you could go outside right now with no consequences, what would you want to do?"

"You know I have been thinking about this for a long time, and it's a tough question because I am very content right now as long as I have you guys by my side. But if you really insist on an answer, I think the first thing I probably would do is just lie down in the grass, enjoying the chilly breeze running between the grass and my face. The sun shining down right on us, the real sun you know. Nothing more, nothing less."

Even in her fantasies, she has a sense of calmness and tranquility. I don't think I have ever seen her unhinged by anything in life. Just always so cheerful and undisturbed. How could I possibly leave her? My constant relief when my thoughts grow so overwhelming and dark?

But instead of telling her any of that, I counter with, "Laaame, well, what I would do is drag you along to the nearest lake and just jump directly into it. Then, I would do a backflip, and we would just have a water fight right there! And I would beat you, of course, as always. But yeah, that's it, though, since it's a bit tougher to splurge with water here. It would be so much fun, I am sure."

She reaches over to stroke her hand through my messy, untamed hair. "I don't know where you're getting your facts from, you rarely win, and when you do, it's because I let you. It does sound like fun, though. Maybe, I could even work on a tan as well after."

We continue snacking until all that is left are small crumbs, and then we pack up and head back home. On the way back, everything is off and deserted. People here all have a systematic way of life for the sake of sustainability, and it has been integrated into part of the culture. But the calmness of the level is what I love most about staying up late.

I feel the whole world is asleep, and the entire level is my own room, where I can do whatever I please and roam freely. I mostly hang out either behind our house, where our field of vegetation lies, or in the central mini grass patch in front of

Jo's store. It doesn't have much but sitting under the lonely tree there gives you the feeling of tranquility, especially at night.

Finally, we reach home, and Odin is sleeping, so we both make sure to make as little noise as possible and head to bed as well.

The following day, I can hear the tractor making some new noises, which wake me up from my sleep a little earlier than I have planned.

"Isim, come here. I know you can hear the noises this contraption is making. Take a look at it and help me out." His words are followed by a loud, impatient grunt.

I rub the sleep out of my eyes and throw my legs over the bed. "Coming, let me just wash my face quickly."

I have a feeling I know what the issue is, and if it is really the fan, I need to fully replace it, which means I need to pass by Jo's store and get the pieces from there. I am a little concerned about who will help him out in the future. Sometimes I feel he breaks his machinery as a challenge for me to fix it. Because it's always a new part that is not functioning well or broken.

I see Sabrina already ready and helping out with sorting the stock into their respective storage spots and packages for later delivery. A lot of people depend on our agricultural goods for their daily nourishment.

I head out to check on our tractor. Even if Odin is secretly creating problems for me to solve, I still love it. Discovering possible solutions to technology-related situations is one of my favorite hobbies. It always feels like a puzzle. I have limited tools, and anything can be solved by utilizing these tools to solve the problem. Makes you think creatively, even in the simplest of scenarios.

I am currently working on an application to automate our orders and keep our stock of goods up to date without effort. It is my final parting gift to Odin before leaving for the upper levels, assuming I pass.

I open up the hood and instantly figure out the issue. I was partially correct, but I need some extra parts from Jo's store to get around the engine. I give the tractor a quick fix so that Odin can keep on working till I get the parts required. I go back to my room to grab my watch and the walkie-talkies for the neighborhood kids.

The walkie-talkies are prototypes I created recently for the kids to try out and give me feedback on their quality. I was hoping to start using it if I were to travel to the upper levels, but the issue is keeping a strong and clear communication signal. I let out a deep sigh; hopefully, I'll get decent feedback from the prototype.

And, for my watch, I simply never leave anywhere without it. It is the only thing I have from my father from before our separation. I wish I knew more about what happened, but all I have are snippets here and there, muddled stories I've burned to memory, relying solely on trust that any of it is true.

One odd thing is the watch is slightly heavy, packed with a tech I do not fully understand. So, for now, it is a device that tells time and is dear to me as the only sentimental item I have left from my father.

On my way to the store, I notice the neighborhood kids. Look at those pesky kids, always looking for trouble. I can tell they are waiting for their next prank to take effect, and it looks like a pretty creative one too. They managed to tie a very light string to two sticks in the middle of the grass, fully undetectable. On one side of the string, it's connected to a pin that would pop a balloon.

That is the perfect diversion because the other side of the string is connected to a release mechanism stretching up the tree branch right above the trap. The release lever would just release a water balloon on the target. A harmless prank, but I bet that would piss off whoever falls for it. I know I'd feel bad if Mr. Jones gets soaked, and I knew about it.

I walk up to the kid's contraption and pretend I don't see it. I can see the excitement in their faces as I get closer, but I stop just one step away from the string and call out for one of them.

"Yo, Lucas! Come here. I have a small gift for you."

His friends stay in their not-so-hidden hiding spot. Right before Lucas takes his last step toward me, I trigger their mischievous contraption. All the kids' attention gets diverted to the popping balloon noise. That is my moment to move aside from the water balloon's fall path and let it swing from the tree branch right onto the side of Lucas's face. The kids are all in shock for a second but burst out laughing the very next second, feeling a mix of victory and defeat.

I place a hand on his damp shoulder. "I'm so sorry, Lucas, but I just couldn't resist. So, to make up for it, I do actually have a gift for you guys."

I can tell he's slightly annoyed, but I can see his smirk as I get the walkie-talkies out for him and his friends. They all come and gather up around him, seeing the new potential toys.

"I hope you guys enjoyed the show. So, as I was saying to Lucas, I got you guys a small gift that I want you to test out for me. I am sure you guys will enjoy it, but I want you to test its limits as payment for them. How does that sound?"

They all eagerly agree and run along to play around with them. I am afraid that this will elevate their troublemaking powers, but it is what it is. Now back to Jo's to get those parts. I enter and wave to Mr. Jones as I go ahead and grab the parts I need for the repair.

"Haven't seen you in a while, kiddo! Studying hard, I bet. Well, I wish you the best on your exam. So what brings you here today?"

I walk past an assortment of tools along workbenches lining the walls and inhale the stale air laden with oil. "Thanks, Mr. Jones. I really appreciate it. Well, I'm here for the usual. Just need some parts for my projects but don't you worry. Soon enough I won't be disturbing you, hopefully."

He cleans his face and then throws the dirty rag over his shoulder. "Disturb! What do you mean? You are my biggest source of income. Please teach some of the kids here a thing or two about your technical skills. You cannot leave me in this state with all these items rusting off. Well, I hope you do visit once you are up there." He takes a second, finishing up with a small part he's working with on a rolling tool cart. "We will miss you, kid!"

I give him an encouraging smile before I start heading back home. I have been reading a lot lately about what the outside world used to look like, and sometimes I imagine what it must've been like to live in it. We mostly have simple products that do not require heavy machinery. Sometimes I wonder how different would life be if we had cars, for instance, to move around.

However, it is unnecessary since this place is not massive enough to accommodate whole bunkers of citizens who own cars. Some people here own bicycles, but they are not too common. We have one at home, but we mainly use it to deliver our produce to those around us. I wonder if the upper levels have better technology than us. I am sure they do, but it is probably used to improve living standards all around.

I arrive home and notice Sabrina already has a patient. Our house is rarely ever empty, we have guests all the time for whatever reason, and Sabrina is the best at what she does. Thanks to her mother's knowledge, it's all so natural with her. She knows the best remedies and the most suitable plants to use as part of her tinctures. It is just unfortunate her mother isn't around to see how great Sabrina has turned out to be. She could cure everything, but no medicine could cure her cancer, sadly.

On the other hand, everyone here is always considerate, and we help each other out without any financial gain. That is one thing I really appreciate about our ground level. We are blessed with the kindest people and enough resources to keep us going strong as a community.

Every week that passes, my levels of anxiety grow. I am confident yet unnerved by the idea that I will be leaving these levels behind one day. It feels like time snaps by in a blink when we finally reach the last week before the big day. I am trying to finalize all my work and projects before leaving. I probably should deliver the produce to our area to get it over with, though.

That way, I can be free for the rest of the day. So I pack up and hit the road on my bike, thinking about all my random projects when, lo and behold, Lucas shows up talking to his friends on the other side of the road.

"Hey, Isim! Thank you so much for these walkie-talkies. We have been using them literally every day, and they have been so useful."

"I'm thrilled to hear that. So any complaints or issues you guys have with them so far?"

"I think the biggest issue we have been facing really is the distance. We have been using them from home most time to plan our hangouts, but Yusuf is the only one who has been having trouble hearing us. The rest of the guys are fine."

"That makes sense. Yusuf does live the farthest away from you guys. When I go to the upper levels, I might find more sophisticated components to build an upgraded version. Sadly, I was limited by what we had here in terms of the quality of the components."

"Yeah, that's alright. For now, they are amazing thanks a lot! I know I still have a few more years until my exam, but I was wondering what are you actually going to be tested on?"

I arch both my brows in response. "You're already excited to leave, I see, huh?" I tease him but then consider the question more deeply. "All I know for now about the test is that it's meant to test your life skill abilities and education in all subjects in school. The idea is to make sure you are the best you can be if we ever get back to the surface. You will learn more as you get older in school, so don't worry too much about it, dude. Anyway, I still need to finish these deliveries, so I'll see you later!"

As I finish my deliveries, I remember that Sabrina wants some medical herbs due to her stock running low. We probably could try to grow them ourselves in our garden, but it will then take space, and it's wiser to distribute the produce among the community anyway. It's an efficient system. It all depends on trust and proficiency in the work. Our heart is in the work.

However, we sometimes need to rely on the upper levels for some other necessities, like medicine and more advanced technologies. All that is usually transported through a modified dumbwaiter meant for all types of deliveries varying in size and heaviness compared to a traditional one only for food or lighter items. I wonder how easy it is to sneak up using it. Doesn't matter anyway; I have my exam soon and need to head home now.

I reach home; deliveries are done; and necessities are picked up. I spot Sabrina working on some of her paintings, a new hobby of hers, but she's doing really well for a beginner. She keeps coming up with creative and artistic projects to work on.

Sabrina beams when she sees me. "Can you guess what this looks like? I know it's not complete yet, but I'm like 80% done."

"It's amazing how even when you're actually almost done, it's still a challenge to try and guess what your work is about." I study the painting carefully, putting together my thoughts before saying, "Well, first, why would you draw Earth as a polygon? I get Earth isn't exactly spherical, but it most definitely isn't a 10-sided polygon either."

"You are pretty close, but that's not the full answer. It's a picture of two things in one. It represents the Earth but also the world we currently live in." She points to different parts of the painting. "This would be the bunker if we were to look at it from an eagle point of view. It's still missing more details to make it a bit clearer, but I thought it was a pretty good representation of the world we live in right now. Especially since it's literally where we lived all our lives."

I nod but then point out, "Except I am not too sure about the first five years of my life. So who knows? I might have lived a lavish life outside these bunkers."

"You wish! If it were a lavish life, you would remember that you were more likely just a damaged robot wandering around, and Odin took you in. It actually makes a lot of sense, no memory before us, good with technology, and apparently doesn't understand art."

"Damn, you're merciless today. At this rate, I might as well stay in the upper levels when I finally pass this damn exam. Goodbye forever."

I walk away, but I know she's smirking at her smart-ass comment. She may have won our banter battle but hasn't won the war. Well, back to work now. I have to put the final touches on Odin's automated stocking application, and I shall present it to him when I get my results.

The week passes by quickly, and before I know it, exam day is tomorrow. What did I even do all week? The usual chores, some work on my projects, and sleep.

Rinse and repeat.

Maybe I'll go for a quick walk again around the neighborhood before heading off to bed. I like to go for walks at this time of night when the lights are off and the world gets quiet and calm. Sometimes I end up walking for hours. Most people would find it unnerving, but I think it's soothing in its own way. Going where no one usually goes.

My favorite secret spot that no one knows about, even Sabrina, is on the rooftop of the secluded grain silos at the edge of our city. There is a ladder that leads all the way to the top where no one usually goes and no one ever suspects someone to be lying down on top of the silos, especially post daytime hours.

I just lie there relaxing and mesmerized by the serenity of the night. Now and then thoughts of my family pop into my head during these long, lonely walks.

I love Odin and Sabrina so much, but I wonder how life would have been if I had my actual parents around with me. Would I still have been so keen on moving upward, would I have bothered doing any projects? Even simpler thoughts, like would I have even turned out to be a night person? No one knows, but I can't wait to meet my dad one day, and I hope I will find him upstairs.

Sadly, I wish I could say the same about my mother, but Odin told me that she passed away when she gave birth to me. Odin did tell me, though, that she was the kindest soul he had ever met. So that's how she will forever exist in my mind, even if I have never had the pleasure to actually meet her. Plus, Odin wouldn't really lie about something like that. However, there was this one time he conveniently 'forgot' to tell me about his badass upper arm tattoo, which I only got to discover by luck when he tore his shirt while working on the tractor.

Anyway, it's getting late, and I think I'll head back home. It's time to rest up in preparation to ace this exam and open up new doors. I bounce on the balls of my feet, ready to take on the challenge.

Chapter 2

The upper-level officials have arrived and have taken over the town's central building, where all the major decisions and meetings are held. They arrived very early in the morning and set up all the necessary equipment. This happens yearly, but I never actually get the chance to see it in person for myself until today. Then, I get to be inside and a part of the whole process aside from the initial setup. I get ready quickly and head to Sabrina's room. She is awake already and covered in paint smudges.

"You're awake? How long have you been awake? Are you ready for today's exam!"

My chipper morning spirit makes her eyes roll. "Wow, relax Isim, I just woke up a bit early and couldn't sleep, so I decided to continue my painting. A couple of strokes here and there, and I will be all done at last. And about the exam, it has no effect on my decision. It would be nice to know I beat your score, though. I will get all the satisfaction I need from that."

I scoff aloud. "Your lack of sleep is making you delusional. You can't beat my scores. I have been revising all subjects all week long, so keep on dreaming. Well, anyway, I look forward to the final product of your art piece. So should I wait for you to go or just meet you there at Central Hall?"

"I am almost done, so if you don't mind waiting? I'll be done soon, and then we can leave. Also, you know you look weird with your sleeves rolled down, right? I am not used to you looking semiformal. You know they won't score you by your looks, right?"

I squint my eyes and roll out my tongue mocking her. I then feel my stomach turn. "Shush, okay! This has nothing to do with it, I just decided to change it up for once. Anyway, I'm kinda hungry. I'm gonna make a quick snack. Want your usual?"

Sabrina smirks and nods in agreement as I leave her room and head to the kitchen. My usual breakfast to go will always be a good old egg and cheese sandwich. This might sound simple, but there is one secret ingredient that many would never think of that makes a massive difference in the quality of the eggs.

When scrambling the eggs, I add a bit of milk to the mix. Makes the eggs so much fluffier and tastier. End it all with the bread toasted with cheese and fresh slices of tomato. Perfect combo. I can never get bored of this meal.

For Sabrina, she likes it with a hint of sweetness. I heard that real honey tasted so much better in the 'before the bunker life'. I think it would have been a perfect addition. For now, we have our own version of fake honey that I drizzle lightly on Sabrina's sandwich.

Taste is really good, but for today, I'll stick to the plain sandwich. Just as I finish toasting the final products, Sabrina walks in dressed in her usual white shirt and beige pants, all cleaned up and ready to go. We both grab our sandwiches and head out.

Everyone is here, both the parents and their kids. As we get closer, I notice the gossip is starting to reverberate all around. Now that the exam is happening, I bet everyone is wondering about the life upstairs and the possibilities of a better life achieved by moving up. I can tell from the anxiety in the air.

I spot a couple of mothers already going around to neighbors distributing sweet snacks. This is not a usual sighting unless something major is happening. I would sneak a cupcake, but I know I would regret doing so right before the exam just in case my stomach starts acting up mid-exam. We finally reach our destination, and Odin is already there, waving at us.

"Why are you kids late? The examiners are inside waiting for everyone to arrive, and they are strict. They do not tolerate tardiness; expectations are high when it comes to this. Start heading in, you two, and best of luck, kids!"

I narrow my eyes at him and take a deep breath. "We are right on time. It's okay. You're always the one that's extra early for no reason. We are heading inside right now, no worries. Just wanted to grab breakfast before going in. See you on the other side."

Sabrina hugs Odin tightly, and we head in, where we are greeted by the two officials with unmoved expressions. They don't seem too happy to see us. The upper levels rarely send more than one person at a time to our level. The fact that we have two officials to supervise and organize the examination process just shows how important this event is. They are very strict on who gets a chance to go to the upper levels and try to minimize that altogether.

Also, I think we are the biggest batch for this year. I doubt it would ever get any bigger since every family is limited to one child apart from the twins in our batch who made it through. That's super rare, and it would be unusual if it happened again, though. After that incident, I remember vaccines were distributed to control the population. Anyway, it's exam time and time to focus. Let's go!

As we enter the room, one of the officials greets us with a chip scanner to our heads. Every newborn gets an implant in their head that keeps their biological data stored in their head. These chips are all disconnected from any other technology and encrypted. With special permission, however, they can be accessed with devices like the scanner gun, but I have never seen it in action or fully understand how they work. A big sign has been posted on the central board of the room. "This exam will be monitored. Cheaters will be dismissed immediately."

My turn comes. I ask as the official does the scan. "Excuse me, sir. So how is the exam monitored?"

The official grunts and answers loudly so everyone hears what he has to say. "As you can all read the sign, the exam will be monitored. The scan will activate anti-cheating measures by tapping into your vision. If anyone came here with some clever ideas, go on. I dare you.

"We will scan your chips again to end the session once everyone has finished. Now, hurry. Move on to your seats quickly." He crosses his eyebrows and points them toward the seating area.

Six hours pass by, the longest six hours in my life. Somehow time passed by sluggishly slow yet fast enough, leaving me with barely enough time to finish everything that was required. I feel fatigued after this extended session, wishing I had eaten something to give me a little sugar rush. They tell us results will come out in the next hour.

Everyone is anxiously awaiting the results outside. I can already see some disappointed and happy faces. Sabrina's expressions tell a different story, though. I can tell she's pretending like nothing happened, but deep inside, it's a big deal. I don't know if it's my gift to read people by their eyes or if I'm just that close to Sabrina, but I don't like seeing her that way.

I reach for her hand with wide eyes. "Sabrina, I have a proposition for you. Whoever scores lower gets to be bossed around by the other for the rest of the evening. What do you say?"

She instantly smirks away. I know I will regret this, but it's nice to see that smirk as evil as it is.

"Deal! You know you lost, though, right?" she says as she shifts directly to Odin.

"How's your back, Dad? It's been a while since Isim gave you a good back massage. I have a feeling today is going to be your lucky day. He'll even take care of the dishes tonight."

Suddenly, the exam building's doors burst open with both officials coming out. One of them stares at the crowd, ready to deliver the big announcement. The other guy heads to the announcement board with the results.

"Everyone, listen up. I will only say this once."

The crowd goes quiet.

"My colleague will now be posting the results on the board. These results are a combination of all the tests that the examinees took throughout the session. The results are divided into two sections. One is the final score.

"The other section will show whether the examinees passed or not. Some might be on the waiting list, so we will reach out to you if accepted. For those accepted, you have two days to mail us a response. That is all."

The officials grab their things and start heading out back to the upper levels. It is like they are disgusted to even be here at our level, rushing to leave while finishing up their announcement. The second they leave, everyone frantically rushes to the board.

I try to stay calm and walk casually to the board but the moment I saw everyone rush, I felt my knees get weak and my arms heavy. It was like they needed to be jumpstarted. I shook it off literally, hopped once, and dashed through the crowd to check the results. My heart skips a bit—there's my name, but not just mine, Sabrina too.

Sabrina sees both our names, looks at me with a wide smile, and raises her arms to hug me. We both passed. Odin emerges from the middle of the crowd, grabs us both closer to him, and squeezes us tightly.

"I knew you kids would pass. Look at you two. You kids are all grown up now. I am so proud of you both. We should head back home and celebrate this major achievement."

We reach home and notice a flavorful aroma filling the house. Odin has never baked anything ever during our time living with him. So it's tough to believe that a real baked good is made by our own Odin. Then, we notice a cake all set and ready on the table in our common area room.

Sabrina's eyes glow as she immediately interrogates Odin. "There is no way this was you! Since when do you bake? Who did you let in to use our oven for this? Is this really a real cake?"

Odin's entire face warms. "I am filled with tremendous pride for you two. I asked around for some tips, but I made it all for you two. I am too old for this, so do not expect me to do this again. I hope it tastes as good as it smells," Odin says as he kindly smiles at us.

Sabrina hugs Odin tightly. "Thanks, Dad."

We end the night on a good note, chatting, laughing, and eating cake. Sabrina did score higher, so I am a man of my word. She doesn't ask for much, but I ended up giving Odin a much-deserved back massage and ending the night by washing the dishes.

The following day arrives. Sabrina has made us all some delicious breakfast, each with their favorite dish in our usual seats at the dining table. We all sit in silence for a bit munching into our meals. Everyone avoids eye contact to not address the elephant in the room until the big question on everyone's mind is finally brought up by Odin.

"Have you two thought about it? What are your decisions on your acceptance? I have an idea of what you two might say, but I would like to hear the final word from the both of you."

I look down for a moment at the food on my plate, my usual sandwich, before answering. "I will miss you dearly, Odin, but I know I will regret it if I didn't go. I am hoping I'll be able to find and reunite with my dad. Or at least figure out his whereabouts. Don't worry though, I will definitely be passing by back and forth."

"How about you, Sabrina? Are you still adamant about staying with us? I will always be proud of you whether you stay or leave, so I hope you make your decision based on what you want."

"Yeah, I don't know." She pauses as she stares aimlessly at the ground. "I will stay here like my mother did."

"You don't have to do what she did," Odin reminds her, and I thank him for it. She needs to know she can walk her own path if she wants. That she can be selfish and dream of things beyond this level.

She doesn't budge. "This level needs me, and I am sure there will be plenty of opportunities to go back up later on if I change my mind."

She says that last statement fully aware it's just a statement to ease the situation. No one has ever gotten a second chance to get back up. By tomorrow morning, we need to send in our responses by mail. So, until then, I've got time to try to convince her and finalize preparations for the move upstairs.

I look to Odin. "Odin, you're a mature man. Have you ever seen the upper levels? Or what do you really know about the upper levels?"

"They have better resources and a better quality of life."

"Come on, we all know that here. You're like one of the oldest people around here besides the crazy old lady, but she doesn't count since she never makes sense. You must have some insider knowledge or hints about the life upstairs."

"How would I know? I am here taking care of my children and this lovely community we live in. Maybe you should try your luck with the old lady. She is actually a lovely lady but misunderstood, that's all."

I am sure he is hiding something, but the question is why and what? I know he said it to tease me, but I actually might go ahead and ask that lady. Come to think of it, I don't know what her name is. For now, I will put the final touches on the inventory management system and head out.

Sabrina barges into my room just as I'm finishing up my work. Her smile is as joyful as it gets, but her eyes say otherwise. She is already dressed up and ready to hit the road.

"I have given you enough time alone. Let's go out for a walk or something."

I roll my eyes. "Sorry, Mooom, I didn't realize we were on some schedule. But, okay, give me exactly two minutes, and I'll be with you. Where did you want to go?"

"I don't care. Anywhere. I just want a change of scenery."

I decide to let her in on my plan. "I actually wanna pass by the crazy old lady. Of course, I have low expectations of a successful conversation. Still, it's worth a shot since I will be leaving anyway."

"Sure, let's go. I heard she's got multiple diseases, and that's why she's in this messed up state. Hopefully, we can catch her today on one of her good days. Let me know once you're done."

I finish up my work quickly and start packing up to head out. Odin is passed out in the living room on the couch. I see an empty plate of cake on the table. Seems like he's having a blast with his latest creation. I will miss these small moments. Sabrina is right outside, waiting for me walking in circles around the porch. I call her, and we head out.

We finally reach the house, which is a mess from the outside, like a haunted house. Windows broken, cracked walls, and worn-out dangling decorations. I am having second thoughts about this plan, but I keep going forward. Can't show Sabrina that fear is getting to me. The door is half-open. I approach it and knock lightly, hoping no one answers, so we can leave.

"Lucy? Come in," a calm voice says from inside.

We step in steadily, hoping not to fluster the old lady. We enter what looks like an ancient library room. Books are scattered all over, accompanied by wool and knitted items tossed all around the room. The old lady is sitting in the center of it all on her rocking chair, knitting. She waves at us to sit on the couch across from her. Her hair is a wild, gray, frazzled mess. The wrinkles along her face spread like webs, but her skin has retained some youth. It's soft, and not at all splotchy.

"Lucy, who is this lovely boy you brought in today *KEEEK*. You look a little different today. It seems like you had *KEEEK* an intense jog today, sweety."

Sabrina responds with no hesitation: "I extended my run today, and I bumped into my old friend Isim. He really wanted to meet you since I always talk about you."

I am impressed at Sabrina's slyness and more so with her poker face about the whole situation. Really feels like she's 'Lucy'. I need to do my part, though, and keep this act going. I wouldn't want her to catch on to our charade, don't want to see her negative side.

"It's so nice to finally meet you, Ma'am. You seem to be as lovely as how Lucy described you to be. You have a… cozy home here as well. How long have you lived here?"

"Did you just wake up, dear? We all moved here a year ago. *KEEEK* And don't call me Ma'am, it makes me feel *KEEEK* old. Just call me Mabel."

People moved to these bunkers in 2062. Her mental state is still living around that period.

"Sorry, I just meant maybe you moved houses. My memory is a bit hazy sometimes, but do you remember how the upper levels look?"

"All I know is they kept taking people from here to the upper levels. No one knows why *KEEEK* or where they disappear to. I bet they decide to stay there *KEEEK* because they can shower whenever they want. Would you sweeties like some tea? I'll go make some."

She stands up slowly and heads to the kitchen to prepare some tea. Sabrina excuses herself to the bathroom. A few minutes pass by, and Mabel is back, holding two cups of tea.

"*KEEEK* WHO ARE YOU, AND WHAT ARE YOU DOING IN MY HOME. *KEEEK*."

Mabel puts the cups aside and throws her slippers at me. Sabrina rushes to us instantly the moment she hears the screams.

"Mabel, it's us. We were just chatting a minute ago. This is Isim. He's my friend I just bumped into earlier. Wanted to introduce him to you."

"Lucy *KEEEK*. Where were you? You can't scare me like that. Sorry about that Isim, nice to meet you. I was just making some tea *KEEEK*, would you like a cup?"

I stumble over my words, slightly on edge and unsure of what to expect from her. "No, thank you, Ma'am. I just wanted to finally meet you and say hello in person. Unfortunately, I have some work to do, and I need to head out now." I stand up to leave.

"That is sweet of you, dear. You look very similar to Zeki. He used to pass by us from time to time, going up and down the levels. Where is he now, Lucy? Do you know what happened to Zeki? He used to always pass by and drop off some snacks from the upper levels."

I freeze up. Did I hear her right? "Wait, Dad... ehm I mean Zeki used to pass by you? When was this? What do you know about him? How did you guys meet?"

Mabel gets flustered with all the questioning and dozes off for a second. Her facial expression changes to a confused face. She looks at 'Lucy,' weirded out.

"Lucy sweety, your friend seems like he's leaving. Would you please accompany him out? I need to go rest for a bit; I am feeling a little tired."

It seems like she has reset again, and I don't want to face that earlier part of her again. I wish I had dared to speak to her a lot earlier. I need to know more about Zeki. I am not used to hearing his name out loud. Well, maybe I can open up this topic with Odin and hear his perspective. We both excuse ourselves politely and leave the house.

Before we leave, Mabel stops us at the door with another strange look, eyeing me specifically. "You have eyes... curious eyes, the kind of eyes that will get you into trouble."

I swallow down the lump building in my throat.

"Yes," she confirms like she sees something in me that I can't. "Be careful with curiosity. It can kill, you know?"

Sabrina pulls us away quickly, but I'm left with those words stained in my head.

That is an interesting series of interactions. If it isn't for Sabrina, I would have never had a chance to get this far with Mabel. Sabrina may still be able to talk to her later on in the future. For now, we start our walk back home, both a little shocked at what just happened but also curious to know more.

We arrive back home, and Odin is nowhere to be found. He must have left to grab some groceries for the week. This is perfect. I can go ahead and prepare his gift. I can surprise him with it the moment he's back. Then open up the topic about my dad or the upper levels. Get to him when he's in a good mood.

I head to my room and plan the setup. I will have everything already set up and a mood notification from the system alerting us that stocks for the carrots are running out. Sabrina notices me setting up a couple of things around, but she has no idea what's happening. Thirty minutes pass by, and I notice Odin getting closer. I settle down on the couch, trying to look casual.

Odin enters, drops all the stuff he got on the counter table in the kitchen, and comes to us in the living room to relax. I sit anxiously, debating the right time to activate the notification. I just go for it. A voice speaks up for the announcement. I never realized hearing my own voice out loud could sound so mortifying.

I prerecorded all the voice lines for the system. It was the only way, but thank god I am leaving, so I don't need to hear myself anymore. Sabrina bursts out laughing. Odin smiles, seeming like he is just about to burst out but is in control.

"Isim, I am assuming this is your doing. Care to elaborate on your latest contraption, son."

"I am already regretting adding my voice, but I might be able to find some way to modulate it to sound less… me. Otherwise, I just wanted to make life a little easier for you since I will be leaving soon. With this new system, you can always be notified when stocks are low, or orders come in. I hope you like it."

I see Odin's face light up with a warm smile. I am not sure if he likes my gift but seeing him smile is all that matters. I am glad this is all working out well.

"So this means you're really leaving us behind, huh? Do I get a gift too? Did you record more stuff for me? Because if you did, I think I'll pass. Thanks." Sabrina finally calms down; her eyes are still watery from all the laughing, though.

"You're such a jerk. Lucky for you, I did manage to grab a gift for you from the disposal bins nearby. Unfortunately, for you, though, it does involve my voice, so you're gonna have to live with it." Sabrina opens her hands with a smirk.

I pass to her my new and improved walkie-talkie 2.0. I am proud of it, and I believe there might be hope for improving its connection further when I move to the upper levels. Hard to properly test it right now without physically being up there. Sabrina accepts the gift, and now my attention moves back to Odin. Formalities are over, and it's time to interrogate him.

"So, Odin, I hear that Dad used to travel quite often between our levels. Care to elaborate on what happened since then?"

Odin's eyebrows rise slightly with an added smirk. He answers directly and with no hesitation.

"I am impressed you actually went to Mabel. I hope she was as lovely as I remember her to be. Sadly, she doesn't remember me too well. Son, all I will tell you is that you should not trust everything the upper levels tell you. Your father used to work for even higher people, and one day he disappeared.

"No one knows where he left or what happened to him since then. The upper levels don't tell us much either. You will do great, son. Just trust your instincts, and good luck up there. I love you, son."

Odin grabs me closer and engulfs me in his warm hug. I will really miss him so much.

I hug him back, granting him rare praise I should have given him earlier, but the words are a whisper, barely audible. "I love you, Dad."

Chapter 3

The travel agents are here, the same officials from exam day, and the town has gathered up with their kids for the grand departure. The agent calls out the names of the finalized list. Everyone says their goodbyes, and we are ready to set off to a new life. Sabrina is still adamant about staying behind, and it seems like the upper levels are not too satisfied with that decision.

One of the agents approaches Sabrina with what appears to be a lucrative offer. Better pay and better perks, but Sabrina remains unmoved by such offerings. A short time later, the agent gives up, and we start moving to become the new members of the upper levels.

I know I shouldn't look back. I should look forward. There's a future ahead, bright and mine for the taking. Not just that, but maybe I'll find my father. And yet, I can't help but peep over my shoulder to look at the world and life I'm leaving behind. The pain swells in my gut, but I only stare a moment before pulling my eyes back to the agents in front of me. My forehead is damp and sweaty.

I can do this. This is good. This is great.

There is a special elevator used for only those with the proper authorization. The agents pull out their ID Cards to activate the elevators for the ascension. We finally arrive, and it is immediately perceptible that we are in an entirely different world. The air somehow feels more processed. Everyone is in awe of the number of vehicles being used in these levels compared to home.

Yet, at the same time, if we were blindfolded, I would have never guessed that cars were being utilized here. I have read briefly about electric vehicles, but I would have never expected them to be this silent. There is definitely less greenery in these parts, hence the air quality difference. Everyone is either busy doing something or in a hurry to go on to their next task.

Everyone is assigned a living space according to the field they will be working in. I will be part of the engineering team. I am not sure yet what exactly I'll be doing, but let the excitement overpower the pain of departing. Everyone is split into different departments. I end up alone, so I quickly decide that I will need to make new friends for my mental health.

I arrive at my house, and it's very clean and basic. So I drop my stuff, relax for a bit, and decide it's time to head out and discover the city around. Let's see what there is to do around these places.

It's almost 5:00 pm, and the place has gotten a lot quieter than when we first arrived. I think work is almost done for most people. I already notice people here are more reclusive than in the ground levels—a couple of hours in, and it's starting to get late. I have checked out most of our area, but I know I definitely need to revisit some spots another time.

We have been given an allowance to start out with before our salaries drop. So I will grab a few snacks to end my night and get ready for tomorrow when they'll give us a quick orientation on how everything works around these levels.

I sleep pretty late the first night. I think it's the adrenaline of starting a new life in a new world. I wake up to the sound of knocking on my door and realize I accidentally slept past my alarm clock. I get up frantically to open up the door. I notice it's someone around my age. I am a little surprised since there aren't many young people at these levels.

"Hi! I am Seven, yes, just like the number. My parents thought I was their lucky child and called me that. I don't mind the name much. Anyway, I am going to be your tour guide for today. Are you ready to head out?" He's slender, in shape, with dark hair that is slightly longer than a buzz cut. Beyond his thick, stylish black glasses, I can see his eyes are blue.

"Sorry, I just need to grab a couple of things; do you mind waiting just a moment? I'll be right with you. You can come in and relax meanwhile," I say, although it is a lie.

I run to the bathroom to wash up and get ready in a world-record time. Thankfully, I still have some snacks from last night's run to the grocery store. I grab some and nod to Seven, ready to head out. It feels like he is familiar with such behavior from newcomers. He has situated himself comfortably in the living area seat playing with some sort of cube toy.

I did not realize it earlier when I opened the door for him, but when Seven stands up, he is at least a foot taller than I am. He is slender and walks with a confident stride. The wait does not shake his zeal toward his mission, either, which I am thrilled about.

I wouldn't want a cranky tour.

Seven beams, clearing his throat before saying, "Our schedule for today is to go around town and to familiarize you with the spots that will be most beneficial to your daily needs. After that, we will pass by work, and you have the option to start on some light paperwork or start tomorrow officially. Any questions?"

"Not an important question, but are you gonna work with me? You generalized the statement, but it feels like you're going to be part of the team?"

"Oh yes, they usually assign people like me to show the newcomers around. It's probably because I'm also one of the younger experienced ones around the office, but I don't mind it. I get an extra paid leave day, so that's nice. Don't tell the others I said that though," Seven says with a wink.

He seems easy and causal. His general attitude helps with any building anxiety inside me. "Honestly, sounds fun, so how old are you then? If you don't mind me asking. Also, that cube you had with you looked cool. What is it?"

"I'm twenty. And you're talking about this thing here? This is something I have been working on to help me out with my fidgety fingers. I made it myself, and each side has a fidgeting function. They're all useless buttons or nobs purely made for fidgeting with," he says as he pulls out his fidget cube and passes it to me.

"That is pretty nifty. Oh, by the way, I just want to give you a heads-up that I actually already went on my own mini-tour around town last night. Are there any locations that are more interesting than the standard areas?"

"Mmmhh. You know what? Yes, I do. I usually have a standard route around to show most people, and they're never as enthusiastic about it at all. So, since you've already gone around, we might as well take a small detour."

Seven changes his path leads the way. We walk in the opposite direction for a while and the more we walked the stronger the smell of love grew. The smell was so strong at one point my mouth automatically started salivating. Just when I thought he was about to pass ahead from the smell, Seven stops, and we enter this really small bakery shop. Seven tells me to wait a moment as he talks to Mila. I can't fully tell what they're talking about, but I see Mila nodding to Seven in disagreement until Seven wins her over, and her expressions change gives Seven and I a smile.

Seven comes over with two muffins in his palms and a smirk of victory on his face. We continue our walk, and he tells me more about what just happened. Apparently, only thirty muffins are made daily, very limited stock for a whole floor, but he managed to charm her to give us a couple using me as an excuse since I am new around here. I am hopeful that one day she will expand her business because these muffins are the most delicious muffins I have ever had. Dare I say, the best in the entire world.

Seven then leads the way into the only major store I have seen throughout the city.

"Okay, random topic switch, but I am going to take an educated guess and assume you're a techy kind of person. Young and working with us in engineering, you must be. And if that's the case, there is this one store that's usually used for industrial or bigger projects. But as part of the engineering team, I come here a lot, but I come even more for personal items," Seven says as we enter the store.

This place is huge and has all sorts of parts for all kinds of devices. I did not know there was such a place. I might find the parts I've been looking for to use for some of my ongoing projects. One thing is for sure; I need to find the right frequency modifier for my walkie-talkie.

"From the looks on your face, I know we will get along well. We still have a lot of time left, so walk around if you'd like and meet back at the counter in, let's say, twenty minutes?"

I nod in agreement and rush around the back to check out the parts needed. The store is around two times the regular size of buildings around here. Almost all buildings have a standard size to maximize efficiency with space, with a few exceptions. I take note of all the parts that I could potentially use later when I'm ready. I finish up and head up to the main counter and see Seven chatting with someone who seems to be the owner.

"Back so soon? I hope you like this place because you'll definitely be coming back for work if needed. Speaking of which, that's our next destination. So let's head there."

We head out to our next destination. I am a little anxious. Meeting people one at a time is fine but being thrown suddenly into a crowd of people is a different story. We finally arrive. We enter the building, and it already feels like the building is empty even though it's a Wednesday. As we pass by the different rooms, I notice each office is occupied with employees working quietly on their projects. I have mixed feelings about this whole vibe.

On the one hand, I am glad that I don't need to meet new people, but on the other hand, working here looks like it will be monotonous. I might have to put in the effort to talk to people and make friends. Back home, I barely put any effort into my social life, and I knew everyone around. We arrive at an empty three-person office.

"Welcome to our office! This is where you will spend most of your time here. My desk is just on the other side, so if you have any concerns at any point, you can just call me. We are usually assigned tasks on the online system. The projects here sometimes vary from physical prototypes to virtual tools. It is our duty to try to develop whatever we can to help the people, from the technical perspective, of course. The more we achieve here, the better we can help the other levels."

I head to my desk and check out my setup. I have my own space and desk with essential equipment such as a computer and fixing tools. I can already tell that I will be spending a lot of time here. And Seven seems pretty chill, so I am glad I have him as my officemate. I settle down in my new office and get used to the setup a little. Seven heads to his desk and starts organizing a couple of things.

After some time passes by, Seven comes over. "I hope you like your office, I did not explicitly mention it, but this sums up our tour. I hope you enjoyed this short adventure. I need to head out now for an errand. Is there anything else I can help you out with before I head out?"

"No, it's alright. I think I have a full picture of how things work around here, so no worries. The best part is that work isn't too far off from home."

"Yup, it's a fairly easy path to work, so you shouldn't get lost. Let me know if you need anything, though. I'll almost always be around the office or so. Take care for now, and I'll see you tomorrow!"

I am all alone now, so I decide to talk to some of the other people around here. Seven is really nice, so the others might be just as nice. I prepare myself mentally and head out to the nearest occupied office. I knock on the door and attempt to introduce myself, only to find I was wrong about my earlier statement. Very wrong.

The person inside the office looks at me for a second when I try to introduce myself. His hand hovers in mid-air, holding the right side of his headphones, waiting for me to finish, so he can get back into his bubble. There is no engagement of any kind except for a confirmation nod at whatever I say. I am not sure if this is the normal attitude around here or if I'm missing something. I attempt the same thing but with another office but with a more enthusiastic tone and approach.

"Hey! I am Isim, and I just started working here. I am new to these levels and thought I'd introduce myself to the team around here. Your headphones and setup seem really cool. Do you mind if I ask where you got those headphones from?"

"Hi. Thanks. These headphones are from that store at the end of the street. I have some urgent work to finish up. Good luck with everything, though."

This is one of the most pleasant conversations I have had around here. Still, everyone seems uninterested in making any conversation at all. I wonder if there are some sort of individualism standards in this workplace or if this is normal around these levels in general. Seven is so different from them, though. I make a mental note to ask him about this later on.

It is getting late, and I am getting hungry. I think I'll grab some food on my way back and call it a night. After today's set of interactions, I already miss home. This sucks, but this is part of the new life here. I wonder how Odin and Sabrina are doing, determined to figure out a way to communicate with them. My walkie-talkie is still not functional between our levels, but I'll work on improving that soon enough.

I head home, eat, and go to sleep a little later.

I think my anxiety is kicking in since it's the first day of work. I wake up super early and can't get back to sleep, rolling around in my bed to try and find a comfortable position. I might as well get ready and head out. I arrive at work, and apparently, I am not the only one there early. It seems like this is normal around here, but still no sign of Seven.

He doesn't give the same 'disconnected from the world' kinda vibe the others do. Whatever, I'll get to work. Before Seven left yesterday, he provided me with a short work guide. I have access to all the required platforms and documents to get started on my work. There isn't much to do around here, so I might as well jump on my work.

An hour passes by without interruption until I get hit by a squishy ball on the head. I look behind just to see Seven pretending to look around as if it wasn't him who threw the ball. I wonder if this is the vibe I attract in friends. Regardless, I don't mind. It's friendly. I just didn't expect Seven to get so comfortable with me.

"Sorry, I couldn't help it. It was too easy, and everyone here is a bit too old to mess around with. How's work going? I can see you're already logged into the task management system. Just want to let you know that these tasks are always tracked and kept up to date. There is no physical boss to keep an eye on you, so you may work whenever you like, as long as the tasks are delivered by the deadline.

"That's all that matters. We never faced any issues except for one specific ex-employee nicknamed 'Bold Bill.' That was before my time here, but apparently, Bold Bill took advantage of this system and pretended to submit his work. With every deadline that came, he became more and more reckless. No one knows exactly what happened to him, but he stopped coming to work one day altogether."

"Oh, wow, do you think he got cast out of the bunker? I mean, I definitely don't plan on going off track with my tasks, but that's still good to know."

"No idea, but I wouldn't be surprised. Where else could he have been taken to?"

That's messed up, but he's right. I worked so hard to get here. I won't let simple tasks get in my way. I still wonder what really happened to that guy, though. What if he's alive somewhere out there? Or what if he was actually sent to the lower levels? But I never realized it was him. Whatever, back to work. He's irrelevant now. I open the tasks page, and it's loaded with some exciting projects. I can't deny how thrilled I am to start, but I can already tell some are more of a heavy load.

Days pass by, and nothing much changes. Life gets very repetitive around here. Go to work, finish up tasks, chill a bit with Seven if he's free, grab some food, head home, rinse, and repeat. I am starting to see why people here become so lifeless, but I can't turn into a zombie like the rest of them.

Sadly, a month passes by with the same tedious routine in a flash.

The road I usually take back home is closed off for some road construction work, so I take an alternate route back home. I never really needed any medical equipment during my stay here, but there's a pharmacy I never really noticed until now on this route. Only then does it click, and I realize it's been at least a month since I've seen or spoken to Sabrina and Odin. I miss them so much; I rush home and check out online guides for how people communicate with the lower levels. It must be a common thing; I am not the first to move to the upper levels after all. I find nothing useful; I think I'll have to wait until tomorrow and check with Seven to see if he knows anything about the process.

The following day arrives, and my body wakes me up super early. I try to get back to sleep but to no avail. I do a couple of stretches and decide, screw it, I'll head to Seven's place, so we can go to work together. I knock on the door. Seven opens, his hair somehow looking messier than his usual even though it's too short to even style it in any way.

He rubs his eyes. "Dude, why are you up so early? I barely got up a minute ago. Now that you're here, come inside and make us one of your sandwiches. I'll go and get ready in the meantime."

In his place, near his bed, are stacks of books. Not just tech books or information that might help him at his job, but adventure books, science fiction, and even some… romance. I tried asking if he was a hopeless romantic, and he deliberately hid them until he became more comfortable with me.

We've become pretty good friends in the last month. He's different from the people in this place, and it still doesn't make sense how that worked out to be. Some time passes, and Seven emerges from his room, all ready and set to go. I am already done with my food, but he grabs his sandwich, and we head out.

"Okay, I'll get to the point. I need to visit the lower levels; how can I start that process? Or even message them at least since I haven't done that in forever."

"Mmmhhh… that's a tricky question to answer. There is a very small post office at the edges of the bunker. No one really goes there, and the guy working there is barely there half the time. We still have time. We can pass by and check it out if you're down."

I nod in agreement, and we head there to check it out. A guy sits there with a sluggish stance, barely aware of his surroundings. The office is so small and hardly has any space for his desk. There is a small box on the desk with a slit section for what seems like envelopes or messages.

A title tag is placed on the desk as well as 'Post Office Manager.' Feels like a trivial thing to have since he is the only person here anyway. He suddenly notices our presence and straightens up, and clears his throat.

"Hey! What are you two doing in my office without a warning or appointment? You know it's polite to knock on the door, right?"

He tries to keep a straight face, but it wears off as he's yawning. Seven smirks and responds right after.

"Come on, George, you know no one comes here. We just wanted to check up on you. My friend here also had a couple of questions. Go ahead, Isim."

"I have already written a message that I want to send to the lower levels. How do we do that? Also, is there a process for visiting the lower levels? I haven't seen my family in forever, and I'd like to visit them."

"Place your message in the box. Just make sure you have some sort of address and to whom you are sending this. I will be honest with you since you are friends with Seven. It is almost unheard of for someone to visit the lower levels. I am just the guide here when it comes to traveling. You need to get approval from the higher-ups to travel downstairs. I will give you all the forms you need to fill out, and I wish you the best."

"As long as there is a way, I will try. Thanks a lot, George. I really appreciate it. I will probably be passing by you a lot now that I know about this place."

I quickly write down all the relevant information for the address and drop my envelope inside the box. George prepares the documents that need to be filled before heading out to the other building for approval and hands them over. I bounce on the balls of my feet, pumped to start the process, but we need to head back to the office. We thank George and start our walk to work.

Unfortunately, this week's tasks require my entire focus. So I will probably try to fill out the forms tonight and pass by the management office tomorrow morning before work.

A few hours pass by, and I don't even notice the time. My stomach starts rumbling, but I ignore it. This happens another two times. I look around to see if Seven noticed or not. He's looking straight at me, confirming that he most likely heard it.

"Dude, an earthquake wouldn't be this loud. Let's get you some food. Apparently, Atef has perfected his falafels, and last I spoke to him, he wanted us to try them out and share our thoughts about them."

Atef's restaurant is one of the most distinctive spots in this whole bunker. It is the only place that serves authentic Arabic food. Atef's falafels are his specialty, but he serves other foods like hummus and these incredible pies. He and his cute wife run the whole store. Even though the community here isn't very sociable, those two are the exception.

One thing I find interesting, though, is that Seven is one of the most affable people I have met around here. Even though everyone in these levels seems to be the exact opposite of Seven, he always manages to talk to everyone as if they're best friends and makes it feel seamless. If I didn't know any better and only hung out with Seven, I would assume that people are actually friendly to approach or talk to.

We are about a hundred feet away when I notice Atef waving at us through the glass wall of his shop. The outer part of his shop is just one pane of glass that lets you see through the whole front side of the shop. We enter, and Atef instantly greets us with a joyous smile.

"Ya welcome, ya welcome, my two favorite customers. I have been anxiously waiting for you guys to come over and give me your thoughts on my all-new falafel recipe. I think this is going to be the one. Go ahead and have a seat, guys!"

"I can't wait, man, but please double Isim's plate. He is here on a mission and ready to destroy whatever you serve him," Seven says with a smug smile on his face.

Atef gets to work directly as we chat for a bit. It's become a habit to chat together since his workplace is pretty much in front of ours. He throws in a few Arabic words with us most time, so we get to learn a few words every visit.

"I always wanted to ask, Atef. How come I have never heard anyone around here speak Arabic? It seems like an interesting language, yet I don't think I have ever seen anyone else who eats here even speak a single word."

"Wait, I never told you? Well, my lovely Hanan and I are the only Arabs in this bunker. We looked around for a while, searching for anyone with close roots but to no avail."

"But there are so many cultures and ethnicities around here. How come?"

"I don't know what to tell you, Isim, but I can tell you one thing. The main reason we opened up this shop was to introduce the community to our culture. If there were anyone with Arabic roots around, we would know if they visited. This way, we spread the love and keep our heritage alive. It has become our way of living now," Atef says as he hands me a single piece of falafel to snack on.

"I am sorry to hear that. Well, on the bright side, I can assure you that you guys serve the best falafels ever and Arabic food in general. These are really great Atef. You have outdone yourself this time!"

As I crunched into the falafel, I felt the crispy outside layer of the falafel burst everywhere in my mouth like fireworks. Crunchy just enough to see the oils sparkle around the falafel yet light enough to not overwhelm your tastebuds. The insides of the falafel just melt in your mouth as you munch through it. Moments later, Atef serves us our dishes.

I would like to say that we take our time eating and chatting, but I go through my plate in a flash leaving no trace of food behind. It all happens so fast. I am hungry and can't control myself around such a delicious meal.

We sit for a bit longer chatting and laughing until it was time to head back to the office to finish up our work. This routine goes on for a couple more days until I finish up all the required documents and files for my visit.

The morning after, I head to the government offices to apply for my visit with all the required documents filled out and ready, only to be rejected instantly for a missing form. I repeat my trip a couple of days later, and this happens again, but a different part is missing this time. It's like they are doing this on purpose, so I get fed up and stop. But I won't stop.

This tedious loop continues for a while with no real progress. The next morning, I pass by the post office. I see George in his usual spot, half asleep. I knock on the door lightly, so he doesn't frantically burst out on me. He wakes up and shakes his head, acknowledging that I'm disturbing his sleep during his working hours again.

"It's you again. Well, since you're here, I have this message for you. It arrived last night. I don't usually receive mail, so consider yourself lucky that you have someone who still cares about you down there."

I smile uncontrollably, take the note, and notice written on the envelope 'From your downstairs neighbors.' I thank George and leave the office instantly to read the message. I rip the envelope open, glad I didn't rip its contents from my excitement.

Dear Isim,

It has been over a month now. Have you forgotten us already? Well, regardless, Odin and I miss you so much. Everything feels so different here without you. I feel it hit Odin the hardest. He has grown a bit tired recently. I am staying by his side, and hopefully, he will get better soon, but you deserve to know. You mentioned in your last note that you are trying to visit, we can't wait to see you! Please keep us updated.

One day we will visit as well, and we must try out those muffins you were talking about. This Seven sounds like an interesting character as well. Oh, and guess what? Mabel actually still remembers you and asks me what happened to you. To be fair, she also forgets she even asked about you mid-conversation, but I know her heart is in the right place at least.
Let's hear more from you! For now, you take care and kickass over there and make us proud!

Best Wishes,
Sabrina and Odin

The longing in my chest crawls up to my throat, making it hard to breathe. I miss them so much, more than I'd ever admitted, and more than I've come to terms with since my time here. If I think too heavily about them, I'll never get anything done. I blink back tears, deciding I need to figure out a better way to get in touch with them aside from this way of communication. I just have to.

Chapter 4

Months pass by to no avail. The routine continues, the frequent visits to the post office never stop, messages are exchanged back and forth, and life is starting to feel meaningless. Is this what everyone feels around here? Why does everyone look and act the way they do? I take a little peep at Seven, and his energy never seems to fade away.

He is working on his project, fiddling with his random toys with the type of energy you'd see in someone who just started their new job. I look back at my screen and try to imagine how anyone can keep doing this routine work and stay content or even optimistic about life. My train of thought suddenly gets interrupted by Seven.

"Isim! Listen, I know the last few weeks haven't been the most exciting times around here, and I don't need to ask you to know. Your face says it all. So here's my proposition. I have a secret location I want to show you. I think you will definitely be intrigued, but we will have to do it by the end of this week after our next deadline. So try to cheer up until then. What do you say?"

I am very doubtful anything is interesting about this place anymore. Still, I will try to keep an open mind. Why would he keep such a place a secret after all? I nod in agreement, and we get back to work.

My workload for this week isn't as intense as Seven's tasks, so I wrap up my work for the day and head out for some dinner at Atefs. I reach Atefs and order some hummus and falafel. It's just me at the shop since I finished up a bit early today, and Atef and I start chatting as I enjoy my meal.

"So, Atef, you have been working here for a while. Tell me, what is the funniest thing that has happened around here?"

"Honestly, people around here are very boring, but I do have one story that will forever stay my favorite and funniest scenario. One day after an exhausting week of work, my lovely wife and I decided we needed a break and went for a quiet dinner somewhere nice for once. It's not something we often do, and I thought it would be a nice change since we are usually the cooks. This one restaurant had a very similar setup to our restaurant, and it was always on our list to check it out one day and try their food. So, we finally headed there. The food was great, and we relaxed for a bit, and then Hanan excused herself to the restroom.

"At that time, I thought there was something wrong with the food. I waited for her for five minutes at first, which later on turned into fifteen minutes. I finally see Hanan coming back, but I notice that her dress has some sauce spilled on it. I asked her, "I am not too sure if I see this correctly, but did you just come from the kitchen? I thought you went to the restroom?

"Guess what happened! Apparently, right after her restroom break, she instantly goes to the kitchen! She totally forgets we are customers there and go into the kitchen to prepare some food till one of the workers comes into the kitchen from the backroom and bumps into her by accident, and that's when it clicked that she was in the wrong place after already being frustrated with me for 'misplacing' all of the items in the kitchen. I couldn't control myself and was laughing out loud throughout our walk back home as she was telling the story."

"Your wife is something else. This is why you guys need to take a break from time to time. Your mind has been stuck in this work mentality forever."

"That was the funniest thing I had ever heard, and I appreciate your intent, but we really like the work. It never really feels like work to me as long as I have Hanan by my side, and I get to do the thing we love the most. Trust me, love changes how you view life. I wouldn't even mind doing literally nothing, as long as I have Hanan by my side."

Their relationship is really cute. They work so well together, but I never thought Atef was this loving and caring; at least, he was never as vocal about it. I begin to wonder if everyone here is holding secrets—things about them that are soft and kind. Why do they hide it?

I shake off the thought.

"So have you met any special girl while working around these levels? You must have at least found an interesting girl!" Atef says as he winks at me.

Honestly, the last thing on my mind, but not intentionally. "I have never really thought of it, to be honest. The people here mostly stick to their work routine and each to their own for the most part. So even if I did, it seems impossible even to try."

"This talk might work with other people but not me, kiddo. I was young once, and regardless of the situation or location, we all want love and to be loved. So tell me it seems like your mind is already on someone, maybe from your previous life in the lower levels?"

"No, not really. I grew up with Sabrina pretty much, and Odin is Odin. The rest of the community is just one big family that cares for each other, but that's all."

"Sabrina, huh…" Atef says as he smirks, trying to incite something but not in a bad way. I brushed it off by not responding for a second, which felt like forever until he continued his sentence.

"Well, I am sure Sabrina is just as lovely as you are since you both grew up together and are very close to each other, I'm sure."

"Yup, she is great, but now it's impossible to even talk to her and Odin ever again unless they somehow figure out a way to come up here. And visits downstairs seem impossible with all the approvals required and the never-ending paperwork."

He gives me a comforting smile. "That is tough; I am sorry to hear that. You are a smart kid. Why don't you create a communication device to chat with the lower levels secretly? It can be as simple as two cups attached to a string to talk to each other!"

"You remind me! I totally forgot about my walkie-talkie, but the ground between the two levels is so thick, though. I doubt it will even work unless I find some sort of alternate way of approaching this."

"Well, good luck, Isim! I am sure you will figure out a way."

I finish up my meal, but before I leave, it hits me. This could be my loophole! "As always, thank you for this delicious meal, but I have an unrelated question. Do you work directly with the food transfers from downstairs? And if so, is the dumbwaiter guarded or not?"

"Mmmm, I do accept the deliveries directly for my restaurant, and I will only tell you because I know your intentions, but please be careful. You did not hear this from me, but there is only one security, and it has become very standard for us to do most of our work unbothered. The security guy takes a lot of breaks. That's all I know, and again, be careful, Isim!"

"Thaaaaanks, Atef. See you tomorrow!"

I exit the restaurant and head out directly to the dumbwaiter location to scout the area and get an idea of where everything is situated. If I can figure out a way in and out of there without being noticed or disturbed, I could potentially make a strong enough link to talk to Sabrina through the vent.

I notice one fascinating detail that might make my life so much easier in terms of access. There is only one entrance to the room where the dumbwaiter is located. This means I can try and monitor the schedule of the guard from afar. I have a plan, but I need to grab some parts from the electronics store to build my tracker.

That week, I plan out everything required to make this work and get to work on it. First, I write down all of the parts that I think I will need to build and upgrade my new gadget. Next, I am building a tracker, and I will attach it to a hidden spot near the only entrance to the dumbwaiter. It will consist of a motion sensor to track the guard going in and out, and I will have accurate timings of his schedule and habits around that area. After that is done, I will need to message Sabrina to meet me near that area to communicate with her as close as possible, so we have a clear signal.

This will be my focus for the week until the hangout with Seven.

The end of the week is finally here, and everything is on schedule. I finish up my work for the day quickly and head out for a quick mission before meeting with Seven.

"Seven, I need to head out for a quick errand, and I'll be back in a bit. You'll be done by then, yeh?"

Seven is in full focus mode on his monitor but nods in agreement. I can tell it's been a tough week, but that's why we need this break, as it's been a while since we hung out properly. I let him work peacefully and head out.

I arrive at the dumbwaiter location. The moment I arrive, I instantly know where to place my tracker. There are some plants near the gate that, at the right angle, I can place my device discreetly and with no issues. I will need to investigate the room's inside later once I manage to get in without being noticed. My task, for now, is done, and it's time to head back to Seven. He should be done with his work by now.

Before I enter our office door, I hear a loud sigh of relief that I can only connect to Seven being relieved of his duties for the day. I enter the room, and I see Seven with a huge grin on his face as he types his last word and clicks 'Submit' with a huge exhale of relief.

He pumps his fists into the air. "I am finally done! What a week! I am ready to head out. Are you ready to head out? Let's head out!"

It's always nice to see him in such a good mood. His fun spirit always reflects on his surroundings in a good way. We both pack up our stuff and head out.

"So what's the plan now?"

"Let's grab dinner, and we can head out after it to the secret location. By then, the city will have calmed down, and everyone will be out of sight. No one knows about this place after all, and I'd like to keep it that way. This way, we will reduce the chances of getting caught or seen as well."

"Wait, so this spot we are going to is illegal? But sure, I am still down. I am intrigued."

"Technically, yes, although there are no exact rules against it since it's a well-hidden spot, to begin with. I am sure people generally are not allowed to go there. Not that anyone would go there but still."

"Whatever, man, I am in. Let's get some food for now."

We grab our usual dinner and chill with Atef for a while until it's the right time to head to the secret location. Seven looks at his watch and then looks at me. He raises his eyebrows, tilts his head, then points to the door—a simple signal that I would get but subtle enough that Atef doesn't even realize. We thank Atef and his wife for the delicious food and head out. The city is as quiet as it can get.

Not a single soul to be seen and no vehicles on the streets. This is already usually the case around here, but more so because it's the end of the working week, and people have gone home to relax—the perfect time for a secret mission.

Seven leads the way through the usual familiar streets. The city generally isn't a huge place. However, certain spots are still not unoccupied for different reasons, such as storage purposes or manufacturing and stuff. Looking at the direction

Seven is taking us, it seems like we are headed to an old storage facility that no one really goes to anymore, almost a forgotten part of town.

There is nothing special about this place. It is near the edges of the bunker walls, with only a few storage building units all connected to each other. We pass by all of them until we reach the right end side of the units.

It is a generally empty lot filled with random junk—tires, bricks, barrels, and even old vehicles that are probably out of service. If you focus and look past all that random junk, you might notice one small circular door with a wheel in the center of it. It looks like one of those doors you see in submarines but rustier. It is obvious that no one has used that door in years or even approached this area based on all the random junk that hasn't even been touched around here.

Seven walks through all the random junk without touching anything so as not to disturb the tranquility of the place. The place smells like an old mechanic garage. Reminds me a little of my small workshop back home at Odin's. A little dusty though, and my workshop only ever gets this bad when I need to tear down the tractor semi completely. I follow Seven into a mazelike path between the tires and old shattered bricks around with no questions until he halts right before the door we saw earlier. I had a hunch that we would eventually head to the door we saw earlier.

"We are almost there. I hope you are not having second thoughts because if so, you better say so now."

My nerves start to take over but also curious to see what's behind the door. I can't think of anywhere this door could lead except to the outside world. Still, at the same time, it's public knowledge that there is only one way out of the bunker, and it is located on the last floor of these levels. Only those with high-level access may even get close to that. However, it's also rumored that those who break the law would be banished through that access. I don't know what to expect anymore, but I am eager to find out.

"Let's go, man. I have been ready for this all week."

Seven spins the wheel of the door until the wheel halts itself. As he begins to pull the door outward, I look into the doorway, and I can tell it's a tunnel but poorly lit because it's really old. There are lights installed into the ceiling around three meters apart all throughout the tunnel. The issue is most of the lights are off or burned out except for an average of every third light. Walking through the tunnel without incidents is possible, but you just need to be generally cautious. Thankfully, Seven came prepared with his flashlight to make our walk easier, so we entered and closed the door behind us.

"So care to tell me what this place is? Where does this tunnel even lead to?"

Seven smirks; I can tell he loves this short moment of power.

"I was wondering when you would break and ask. I am impressed you kept calm up until now. I will start by saying again that this place is a secret spot, and no one really knows about this place since it's been kept on the down-low for years now."

"Dude, if I were to tell anyone, it would be you. It's not like I have made tons of friends around here. But, okay, continue, I'm listening."

"Let us start with a short history of this place. So you know about the main gate to the outside world upstairs, right?

My grandfather apparently was one of the first workers to help out with this bunker project. He was part of the construction crew that helped build every part of the tunnel, so he knew every nook and cranny of this place by memory. This information was passed along up until me.

"So, when they were building the main gate, part of the plan was to make a backup gateway in case anything was to ever happen to the main doors. I am sure the governing levels upstairs know about this place, but it was just never needed, so it's been ignored for years."

"Oh my god, no way! So, technically, we can actually go and run into the outside world freely?"

"Sure, you can, but I wouldn't recommend doing that since the world is still a noxious and unsafe place. I even heard the creatures living outside have mutated and turned into monsters that would kill on sight, but I have personally never seen those."

We keep walking for about ten minutes straight. The tunnel has this chilling effect where you feel like you are always being followed or stalked. Insect-like sounds surround us as we walk forward, but we can't see much. I bet this is where most of the vermin population resides since they are hardly ever disturbed around here. I wouldn't be surprised if some of those vermin snuck through some holes or vents around here.

We finally arrive. I didn't realize we have reached the end until Seven points to the door ahead of us. I have been too distracted trying to spot the potential rodents around us but to no avail. Whatever. As long as they don't come near us, all is good.

Seven pulls down a small lever that triggers a loud noise from the room beyond the door. Seven explains that it's the air filtration system doing its work. The door is another one of those pressurized doors with a wheel handle. Seven starts to spin the wheel, and we enter the next room.

"So what do you think? Obviously, we will not leave, but isn't it so cool to be so close to the outside world yet so far away? Take a look and let me know if you spot anything interesting. I once spotted a wild rabbit, but that was the most interesting thing I have seen," Seven says, pointing toward another door. One that was at the other end of the room with a see-through window to the outside world.

I look out through the window, chills going through my body as if a strong cold breeze brushes right through. It feels surreal that the real world is right in front of my eyes. I take a deep breath while fully submerged to my own outside-world fantasy but all I can get is the smell of old metal and dust from the window edges.

I look around outside to see what the world has become or if any creatures are even around. The outside world looks normal as if nothing happened, at least according to the pictures I've seen in books. I see trees and bushes swooshing around with the wind, and it's so mesmerizing to look at. I try to imagine the sound the wind is making as it hits the branches and leaves around.

"He… o… elo… Are… ou… there… ello?"

A small voice calls, but I can't tell from where. There is no one outside the window, and I instantly look back, and I see Seven playing around with the suits.

"Did you say something? I heard a voice."

Seven gives me a firm glare. "What are you saying? There is no one around here, but check out these cool suits. Do I look like an astronaut? They're so heavy, but I've always wanted to try them out."

What the hell am I hearing if no one is around here? I must be imagining stuff. The suits look pretty cool, though, so I go back to Seven to check them out more thoroughly.

"It's the oxygen tanks, man. The compressed air makes it so much heavier than I expected. Look, even the helmets are so damn heavy. Are they supposed to be this heavy? Damn," I say as I try on one of the helmets.

"Yooo, Isim! I can hear you. That's so cool. These helmets are all connected by some auditory system. I have always come here alone, so I never realized that."

"Man, do you think we'll ever get a chance to walk in the outside world? Have you ever thought of taking a walk and coming back, maybe?"

"I don't know, but I know that these doors will probably alert the higher-ups, and they would figure out if the outside door has been accessed. So, if you ever open that door, you better be ready not to come back again!"

I hope we can actually live outside again in our world one day, but he's probably right. If these doors are connected to the bunker systems, and we are discovered, there is no looking back.

We keep on chatting for an hour or so and mess around with the suits until Seven starts yawning. It's almost past our usual bedtime. It's time to head back, but it's been a long and fun day. Just before I am about to close the door behind me, I hear the voice again.

"Isim? Is… t… at yo… name?"

"Who's there? Show yourself!" I respond instantly. We spent an hour in here, and there is no way anyone could have gotten inside during our stay without us knowing. This time I was a little bit more attentive and realized that the voice was close to me. I am not 100% sure, but it really seemed like the voice came from my watch. It is either that or someone hiding underground because the voice was too low.

I get no response. It is late, and we are both a little tired. I close the door, and we head back home, but I can't stop thinking about that last thing. I am positive I heard a voice talking, and on top of that, it knew my name. How am I supposed to sleep with that voice in my head?

"Everything alright, buddy? You seem pretty distracted, zoning in and out. No one knows of this place, and that voice couldn't have come from outside. I am sure it's nothing. Let's get you back home, and you can sleep it off and relax this weekend."

I am not convinced by what Seven says, but I agree with him nonetheless, and we continue our walk back home. Once I reach home, I prepare to head to sleep, but the moment I get in bed, my mind gets louder with thoughts about today's incident.

I am sure I heard those voices from earlier, and the fact that the person knew my name made it even more intriguing. I take my watch off my desk and start inspecting it. I have worn this watch every day ever since I got it. I always knew that this watch was no normal watch but didn't think it could be some sort of communication receiver for a second. Assuming the voice I heard really did come from my watch, all I can think of right now is that the person on the other side is currently living outside. I must have been so close to some communication tower on the outside that it made it feasible to receive a signal.

I need to go back to the tunnel and check if my theory works, and if it does, then this means there is hope that the outside world has become habitable again. I need to tell Sabrina about this as well. It seems like I have plenty of work on my plate these coming weeks.

I think I need to keep these thoughts on the down-low for now until I confirm everything. What if my father is living on the outside? Maybe that's why he's nowhere to be found even on these levels. I need to figure this out!

Chapter 5

It is Saturday already. Saturdays are usually my alone days when I relax and am free before getting back to work. After last night though, I can't relax. I have barely slept last night. I lie in bed staring at my ceiling for hours on end, going through the possibilities of what's happening in the outside world. Does my father have anything to do with this? Do the people higher up even know something we don't know about the outside world?

Tonight, I will be going back to the tunnel and try to talk to the voice again. I am 90% sure that it is coming from my watch. The watch is very delicate to tinker with, and I don't want to mess around with it too much, but I can tell what some parts do. For instance, I detected a voice receiver in the watch for sure, so it has the potential for communication through the watch.

I also need to plan my visit to Sabrina, but to do that, I need to be patient and gather more data on the habits of the guard and the location itself.

I finally gather up the power to get out of bed. I wash my face and head to the kitchen for a quick snack. I see I still have one last muffin in the fridge that would be perfect right about now. I heat it up just enough for the chocolate chips on the inside to reach melting point. As I am munching on my snack, I realize I haven't updated Sabrina on my latest plan. So I grab my notebook and start composing my message.

Dear Sabrina,

I do wish visitations were easier. It's been forever since I last saw you guys; I miss you guys. You know, if I had an arch-nemesis, I still wouldn't wish it on them to visit the lower levels with this dumb application system, but I think I have a plan around that. I know the walkie-talkie I gave you doesn't allow us to speak across levels, but I think I have a plan to fix that as well.

I need you to keep an eye on the dumbwaiter for me. That could be our gateway for communication. I know no one usually cares about it down there, but just in case. I will update you further next week after I collect enough information about my end of the dumbwaiter.

How is Odin doing? I remember you last told me he was a little sick I hope he's all better now. Take care of him and yourself, Sabrina!

Regards,
Isim

I'll drop it off tonight before I check out the tunnel. I have been thinking about what Atef said previously about the cups and string. That is the original communication device, but this won't be a feasible solution with the distance between my end of the dumbwaiter and the lower level.

But it's really a good initiative for a more modern approach. I might sneak a connection wire between the elevator and the shaft at the edges. It's perfect since gravity will just help me slide it to the bottom. Sabrina would need to look around to find it, though, but it should be fine.

I will need to allow for the wire to be plugged in through the walkie-talkie's charging port to allow for data to be used through that port. It's the only way and will do the job. This will be my project for today. I'll pass by the shop and grab all the tools and equipment required to finalize this mini-project.

A few hours pass by like it's nothing. I have shopped for the required pieces and tools, fixed up a small prototype to test, and then made some food for lunch and dinner into one big meal. It isn't on purpose but I ended up with a lot of cooked pasta, so I kept eating.

I never know how to measure the proper amount of pasta for any specific number of people. I just throw an estimate of what's enough and hope for the best. Anyway, it's almost time for my trip. I search for my flashlight, so I can head out.

The streets are quiet at around this time. Most people are preparing for the next day of work. The streets are never this quiet, usually in the lower levels. I have always found that fascinating since the moment discovered that. As much as I love the serenity of these levels, I still miss the lower-level vibes.

There was rarely ever a moment of silence. Even late at night, when everyone was mostly asleep or preparing for work, you'd notice children messing around just outside their homes, avoiding sleep. You could even notice through the window's shadows, kids running back and forth in their own homes. I miss these little snippets of life.

I reach the post office to drop off my note. George is barely awake as always. He notices someone is in his office.

He squints at me as if he's trying to make sure it's really me, then takes a quick glance at his watch. The moment he realizes what time it is, his eyes widen with joy.

"It is you again. How many times have I told you to make an appointment before coming over? It is almost closing time now!" George says in his usual tone, trying to sound affirmative but somehow not too convinced in what he's saying.

"Soooorry, George, I promise you that I will try to not bother you so late in the day. I just have a note to drop off for today, so I won't keep you for long," I say as I drop off my message in the usual box.

"Okay. I will allow it this time, but you better this does not happen again." George says nonchalantly as he stands up, packing his stuff to leave.

I feel like I have turned into Seven, I got used to the people around here and learned how to handle each person. George and I have a special relationship where we are not exactly friends but have our little banter every meet-up.

I usually would make more small talk, but I must keep it short this time so George can close down early and head to my quest. I excuse myself and say goodbye.

I arrive at the storage units anxious, trying to keep my head straight as I walk through the junkyard and take short glances at my watch if something turns on. The moment of truth, I am at the first door. I swing the wheel of the door and pull open the door just enough for me to pass through and close it right after. It might be because it's my first time opening this door, but the door is heavy. Seven made it look so seamless when he did it last time.

The moment the door is closed behind me, I hear those same sounds of vermin scurrying away from around me. I make a secondary torch light attached to a headband to always have a light source in my peripheral vision.

The closer I get to the second door, the more anxious and attentive I get to my watch. I keep mishearing voices coming from the watch. What if I really am hearing stuff coming out of the watch, but just can't tell. I need to get inside soon.

I open up the second door and enter—the moment of truth. Silence ensues in the room. It feels like I am stuck in space and time. No sound or even movement from the usual suspects. It's like time itself has paused itself just because it knows how anxious I am right now. A minute that feels like forever passes by without a single disturbance in the room.

Maybe this was all in my head. Maybe I should just dismiss this thought altogether and go back home and sleep. I approach the outside door to look at the outside world one last time before heading back home. The trees and bushes look as calm as ever. Still no sign of life. Maybe I was too optimistic, thinking there might be life outside.

"Isim… Is that you?" a familiar voice says.

"Hello, yes! Who's there? Hello."

"Zel… Here," the voice says, coming from my watch.

"How do you know my name? And where are you talking to me from?"

I realize that maybe the connection is still weak, so I bring the watch closer to the window, hoping it could help the connection even if slightly.

"I heard… your name being called… more than once. I assumed… that… that was you. I am not entirely sure… I have been living here for the longest time."

"Are you in the bunker?" I say as I notice it starts to drizzle. I imagine it, falling down and hitting the ground with gentle thuds.

"No… but there… greenery… around… And… the cabin… nice."

Her voice keeps getting interrupted as the rain gets heavier. After that last sentence, everything else becomes gibberish.

"If you can still hear me, the connection has become very weak from the rain. We will have to continue this later on. Take care, for now, Zel."

I hate having to end this right after communicating with her, but I really can't make sense of anything she's saying now. I might try to install an add-on attachment to the watch to improve the signal. It should help out even if it rains next time.

I turn back and march back home. Excited, relieved, sad, and hopeful. I wish I could talk more; I have so much more to say and ask. That last interaction just raised even more questions. She said there was some greenery around, I think.

We have some greenery here, but the fact she said it combined with a cabin as well. It does not point to anywhere in here. She must be living on the outside, and the fact that I can hear her best when closest to the outside world proves that she's living outside somewhere.

She must have either figured out a way to live safely from the toxic air or the potentially vicious creatures. What if the air got better and the mutated creatures are friendly animals that just got unlucky? Is she alone out there also? She can't be too far away from the area if the communication towers allow us to talk. She might even stumble into the bunker doors and see me. My mind won't stop thinking of all the potential possibilities.

I reach home to prepare myself for sleep but little did I know that my mind would take over. Eyes burning yet wide open with excitement thinking about potential hope outside the world. What if my father left for the outside world and met Zel? If he did, there might have been deeper reasons for keeping it a secret. I can't be sure of anything yet, but the thought of it all kept me for a couple of hours before I could finally sleep.

The next morning, I wake up slightly earlier than my scheduled alarm. I try to sleep it off, at least until my alarm actually goes off. Exhausted and in bed, but sleep never approached me during that period. I decided I might as well get productive. I prepare myself and leave the house a little earlier than I usually would, heading straight to get more parts for the watch upgrade from the electronic store.

I finally arrive at the office after my quick detour, but Seven is nowhere to be found yet. The first day back to work is always a lazy day, so I'm sure he overslept. This is my chance to finish the watch upgrade before he arrives. I sit down with the parts I just got and start working.

I don't know if I should tell Seven about this. I have been debating the thought for a while. I might tell Seven once I clearly connect with Zel and gather more information about her whereabouts.

Seven arrives an hour later with some fresh muffins and a grin. You can tell he's proud of the early trip he'd made to get those muffins. He walks over to my desk and drops the tray of muffins on it.

"I was literally the first person there. Man, the fresh smell of those baked goods alone was so worth it! Since I was the first there and no one was there yet, she gave me a free muffin fresh out of the oven, and it was so delicious. Slightly crispy on the outside but soft on the inside that when you attempt to chew through it, it dissolves on your tastebuds."

"Aw man, I wish I joined you! This sounds so good. We need to go together next time." I exclaimed back but knowing on the inside that my mind was still all over my recent discovery.

I grab a muffin and get right into it. I can never get bored of them. Almost makes me feel like I want to stay in these levels just for this. Seven is so preoccupied with a book in his hand this morning that he doesn't look too much into my work and walks toward his desk to start his own work.

Hours pass by like a breeze. I finalized the upgrade and finished a couple of tasks from work. Today has been a successful day of work. Seven stands up, stretches his arms, and jumps onto our recently created bean bag with a sigh of relief. Bean bags are generally a luxury around here. We made this one ourselves with some fabric and dry uncooked rice. It turned out pretty well.

"So I never asked you, what did you think of our last trip? Hope it was an interesting experience from our usual dull days around here," Seven asks.

"It was very interesting actually. I was thinking, though, what if there were people outside. Would you ever consider leaving this place behind us and try to live outside? Ever since our last trip, I have been thinking of that. Aren't you at least curious if there's more to life than just this tedious routine we are living in?"

Seven lets out a cautious sigh, and a flicker of doubt crosses his features. "Listen, I am always down for new adventures, but this doesn't sound like a smart idea. First, we don't even know if the world outside is habitable, and assuming it is, what would we even do there since no one lives outside?"

"You make a good point, but what if people are living outside and this whole bunker life is a sham? Maybe we could be the pioneers in the new life outside. I know there are secrets out there, especially since I still can't figure out much about what happened to my father or his whereabouts even."

Seven shakes his head up and down in a semi-skeptical way and with a hint of agreement. Thinks about it for a couple of seconds and responds.

"You know it's not a horrible idea assuming everything you said is true, but it's not an easy thing to do. On the other hand, it does sound interesting as a thought… for now."

We end the conversation at that, and both get back to work. Our week just started, so each person has their own work and deadlines to meet. But it is definitely not a decision to take lightly. This is why I need to go back tonight, talk to Zel and learn more about her.

Six hours pass by. Seven and I both worked almost continuously since he got to the office with a couple of chatter interruptions from time to time. Time passed by so quickly in my mind. It might be because this whole time, I've been thinking about the next steps with Zel, Seven, and Sabrina.

We wrap up work and have our usual dinner at Atefs. It is a good way to waste time till I have to go back to the tunnel. We walk back to our apartments and split from there until the next day, Seven thought. I head inside, grabbing a couple of things in preparation to head out to the tunnel.

I take the usual path with the usual vermin companions scurrying around me as I walk through the tunnel. Finally, I arrive inside, past the second door, and shut the door behind me. I look outside the window. Thankfully it is not raining, so there should be no issues anymore.

"Zel? Hello, are you there?"

Silence ensues in the room for a couple of minutes until finally, a voice talks back. It is a lot clearer now after the recent upgrade.

"Isim, you are back! It is lonely around here, so hearing your voice is nice. Your voice seems clearer as well. How are you doing?"

"At last! I can finally hear you clearly. I have so many thoughts and questions that I need to ask you! But I am doing well. How are you doing?"

"Better now that we can finally communicate clearly. I miss talking to people. It has been a few years since I last spoke to anyone, really. So I am all ears. What are your thoughts?"

"You used to speak to someone else? What happened to that person?"

"I cannot remember much past a certain period of my life, but I remember the time he entered my life. He was very kind and lovely. I couldn't see him, but he talked to me the same way you are right now. He checked up on me almost every day until one day, he just disappeared. I haven't heard from him since. His voice felt familiar, but again, I couldn't tell who it was exactly. He told me his name was Zeki."

I open my mouth to ask when that was, but my mind is in control, and not a single word comes out for a whole minute. This can't be a mere coincidence. Something happened. Zel finally breaks the silence.

"Isim, do not tell me you disappeared too. Is everything alright?"

I struggle to find the words, pulling them from my throat with great effort. "Yes, yes. Sorry, that is my father's name, and I haven't heard his name spoken out loud twice in a row by a random stranger that I don't know."

"Oh, I am assuming he isn't around either. Well, I hope he is doing well. He was a nice fellow. I enjoyed his company very much. Anyway, how about you? Where are you right now, and how come you are the only person that can talk to me?"

"Well, we all live underground now. It feels like you are living outside. Is it true?"

"No wonder no one is around here. Why is everyone underground, though? I had no idea."

"How do you not know!" I exclaimed.

How can she not know? She either is inside the bunker or outside of it, and I am sure she is not around here, so she must be outside. This just proves there is more to the outside world than we are told.

"The world has become a toxic place apparently and is no longer a livable place anymore. Though the fact that you've been living outside for a while now, makes me doubt if that ever was the case. Or maybe the state of life got better with time. It is even said that mutated creatures live outside that attack on sight."

"I have not seen any weird creatures personally and have been living normally with no issues. I tend to my garden daily with no issues," Zel responds in her very usual relaxed tone as if the news I just deliver means nothing to her.

I pause for a moment collecting my thoughts. My mind is all over the place but blank simultaneously. It's an odd feeling because I want to know more about nothing else that's important right now. She is living life as if nothing happened outside, she has no idea of what happened to the world, and we are stuck in this underground world of ours. I finally gather up my thoughts and remember my father's topic.

"Well, back to Zeki… my father. When was the last time you heard from him?"

"I stopped keeping up with time as much around here. I am sorry, but I think the last chat I had with him was around two years ago. Feels like ages. I have been alone ever since."

"Okay, so tell me then. How was my father? What did you guys talk about? Tell me anything, really. I was too young when he left, and I barely know anything about him."

I sometimes wish I could just have five minutes with him just to feel like I had a genuine and memorable connection with him. Right now, all I have are vague memories as a child and this watch that I can only cherish even further after this recent discovery.

"I have not seen him, but he was like my caretaker. He was always around, in voice, making sure everything was alright. He would say, 'Just be patient, and life will find its way to you' if I ever needed anything. And it usually did! I can swear sometimes he could perform miracles if I ever desired something that was not as easily available. I used to try to grow some strawberries for a while but always failed.

One day, after bringing up the topic, I found that my strawberries finally sprouted and were in good shape. How about you then, do you like strawberries?"

"Thankfully, I love strawberries. They're one of the fruits that are fairly easy to grow anywhere and in any climate as long as you have enough sunlight. Which, of course, we managed to replicate the sun rays for agriculture artificially."

We kept talking for the next hour and a half about the most random stuff after that. As much as I wanted to know about the outside world, for some reason, talking to Zel didn't feel like I was missing out on much I didn't already know. Assuming the outside world is actually normal.

It feels nice to talk to a new friend. Seven is my most recent friend, and he is interesting for sure. However, with Zel, there is a lot of mystery and ambiguity since she lives outside and can't ever see her unless I go outside. A part of me seems interested to know who this person is that my father cared for so much.

She is nice, though, regardless of anything. I get to know more about her with no effort. She loves to chat about literally anything, and she is good at it. After an hour and a half, I learn that she likes pies, all animals, books, and long walks and hates dishes.

"So, by the way, it's getting late here. I'll come back tomorrow for sure, and we can continue our chat. I need to wake up early for work. Now that we can finally chat clearly, I can come over for a chat every night or so. So take care for now, and I'll talk to you soon!"

"Take care and talk to you soon!"

I pack up my stuff and head out back home with a new feeling of superiority. I know something that the whole world doesn't. Something I am not sure if I should share with the world. I might get called crazy. And if I dare show them proof with my watch, it will be taken away from me, and I can't let that happen. So, for now, I will need to keep it a secret until I figure out a smarter way to handle this.

I start my amble back home, but this time, something is different. My view of the world has changed. The alleys and streets feel darker than usual. The paint on the walls of the houses feels worn out, so I can tell the silhouettes of the walls brick by brick. I didn't get to learn much about the outside world, but those fragments of life described by Zel were enough to shake my world on the inside.

The big question remains, though. Where is my father?

Chapter 6

This time, I am first in line to get those baked goodies. The room's aroma overwhelms you in a way that feels inescapable and in just the right ways. The scent feels very visible as it enters your nostrils and sneaks its way just to lay down right on your tongue to give you a sense of what the muffin would taste like. I see Mila approaching me with my order. I take my order and head out to the office.

The moment I enter the office, I immediately feel a sense of déjà vu, except the roles are reversed this time. I walk over to Seven and nod to him with a smirk. He immediately smiles and knows instantly what just happened. We happily munch on our baked goods and continue working for the rest of the day.

For weeks on end, life has been dull and more so after moving to the upper levels. It saddens me to realize that I'm blending in as part of the society here. The aura of this place seems to consume the life out of you bit by bit. Like a leech, covertly absorbing every drop of blood out of your veins until it is pointed out to you by a bystander.

Even though Zel didn't point out anything specific, she still managed to re-ignite my enthusiasm around here. It's been so interesting to get to know more about Zel and life outside. It has only been ten days since we first spoke, yet it felt like more. Lately, I have been contemplating the thought of going outside myself.

However, such a decision would have serious consequences that I am not sure I am willing to risk. It could mean that I would never come back, which also means never seeing Sabrina, Odin, or Seven. This is why I need to tell them about these discoveries as soon as possible, starting with Sabrina.

Enough time has passed to know the schedule of the guard. I need to move to the next part of the plan. The plan for tonight is to collect all the data from my devices about the guard. Then I need to write to Sabrina about a suitable time and place to meet based on the data collected. I might be able to convince her of life on the outside.

I know Sabrina well enough, though. I know that she wouldn't even leave the lower levels to begin with, and to top that off, leaving the whole bunker into the outside world. I would still love to try regardless. Honestly, just sharing my discoveries and chatting in person is enough for me.

I think I might drag Seven along for when I meet up with Sabrina. This way he can finally meet Sabrina, and he can keep an eye out for the guard in case he gets off track with his routine.

For now, I will leave the office just before working hours are officially over to gather the data from my trackers and be back in time.

"Hey, Seven, do you want anything from the supermarket? I'm going to get some snacks, and I'll be back."

"Actually yes, get me some of those salted chips. The plain ones, okay, don't forget!"

I head out and start reminiscing on my way to the dumbwaiter location about my old life at the lower levels. We used to be the starting point in the production of those chips. We grew those potatoes ourselves in the lower levels, cut them up, and salted them. I managed to automate most of this process, but it came from our hard work, and it's all done in the lower levels. Sabrina and I used to always pass by the food storage unit and get free samples of the new products to be distributed. I miss those days.

I reach the location, and no one is around. I made a wireless tool to collect the data discreetly. All the required data has been collected. I grab some snacks from the supermarket right after and head back to the office.

I drop off the snacks to Seven and head directly to my computer, back to work. I am so excited to see the results, so I can start planning. My eyes widen in excitement as I realize that the guard is very systematic with his break routine or whatever he does during that off period. Apparently, every day he disappears for an hour at 1:00 pm and at 7:00 pm. In some cases, it even extends to an hour and a half.

"Hey, dude, what are you grinning at? Did you get a fun task behind my back? Yalla, spill it out." Seven says using a new word we learned recently from Atef, 'yalla' meaning 'let's go'.

I nod my head toward my computer. Seven understands and comes over to my screen. I fill him up on the details of the plan and my recent discoveries.

"Damn dude, you have been working hard on this. You are gooood. You kept it on the down-low for a while as well, and I had no idea. I felt there might be something but didn't think it's this deep."

"So you really think your dad might be outside based on your last interaction? Dude, if it's really true, we need to go outside. What if we get to be the first humans to move civilization forward to the outside world? We will be remembered in history! Okay, so what's the plan right now?"

"You know messages are usually sent every month, but I think I got a quick fix for that. George owes me. I actually passed by him earlier and dropped off a fresh muffin. So, I think I can persuade him to send my message to Sabrina early just this time, and it will be the only time needed anyway. I am planning to drop off my message later on today, and he will hopefully send it by tomorrow. I will give it some buffer time and plan to meet two days after tomorrow, so she can get it in time, and we could meet."

"Wow, you really got it all figured out. Well, count me in, anything to get me out of this tedious routine we got going, and plus I would love to meet this Sabrina of yours finally," Seven says with a smirk.

We discuss the plan further and decide that the evening timing would be best for the meet-up. It is settled. All that is left before our meeting is setting up the connection I had devised for communication beforehand. This way, we can utilize our time as efficiently as possible during the meet-up.

Official working hours are over. I have written out my message to Sabrina and am on my way to drop it off at the post office. The moment George and I make eye contact, George's face is beaming for once. I don't remember him ever greeting me with a smile. The moment I bring up needing a favor, it's like his emotional settings just got reset to his previous default—back to his uninterested expressions and banter.

We agree on the delivery to be done, and he prompts me as usual to not repeat this, but it's all part of our banter. I will definitely be dropping off more goodies on my next visit as a thank-you token. Wouldn't want to get him on his bad side in our relationship.

It is currently 7:15 pm, so it's time to head to the dumbwaiter to install the communication cable I devised. I arrive to find no one around, as expected and then proceed inside the building unit. The room is as big as three cars side by side. There is already one small truck parked on the side, which I can only assume is used to deliver bigger items if ever needed. On the other side of the room, there are a bunch of different boxes and a dedicated box cart on the side. I start walking forward toward the dumbwaiter doors.

I feel a rush of adrenaline as I take a look inside the dumbwaiter. I am so close yet so far away from being able to move freely between levels. The elevator makes loud moving sounds, so if the guard is outside, I would definitely get caught. That is assuming I can even get past the security panel to activate the dumbwaiter.

For now, I need to stick to the plan. I grab the rolled-up cable around my waist and start sliding it down the side of the elevator shaft. I brought a small hook with me that can be screwed into the walls of the shaft. Turns out I don't need to drill anything into the walls of the dumbwaiter.

I get lucky here, but there is one screw from the metal panels that is accessible. I unscrew that and replace it with the hook I brought to keep the cable hanging out of sight from anyone who generally uses the lift. I tug my cable end to the hook and leave it as is for the next time back.

I need to leave before the guard is back. Now all that is left is patience till the day of the meeting.

The days pass by with the usual routines. Go to work, get food, and head home. Today is the day we finally act on the plan, though. Seven and I finished all our work for today, and it's time to head out. We start our walk to the location.

As we are walking toward the location, we notice the guard actually walking toward us away from the direction of the dumbwaiter area. This is the first time I see Seven ignoring a person around here. He never ignores anyone, and he knows everyone around here. There is always some sort of interaction between him and others, even if it means a simple nod or smile.

We both enter the dumbwaiter building unit and rush directly to the shaft. I have instructed Sabrina to look around from her end in the shaft for the cable and connect it to the bottom of her walkie-talkie that I gave her before I left. Hopefully, there shouldn't be any issues.

I grab the cable I tucked previously and plug it into my walkie-talkie. Seven stares at me with a spark in his eyes and nods toward the walkie-talkie to proceed.

"Hello? Sabrina? Seven and I are here. Are you connected?"

"Isim! Oh my god! It has been forever since I've heard your voice. How are you?"

Her voice is like music to my ears, and I'm flooded with a hundred warm memories. "It has! It's all good here. I am glad you managed to find the cable. I was a little unsure if it would be accessible from your end. By the way, Seven is here with me also."

"Hey!" Seven responds in excitement.

"Took me a couple of minutes to figure it out, but I managed no worries. And hey, Seven! I've heard so much about you. I hope Isim has been treating you well. Let me know otherwise. I am not around anymore, so I am sure he's out of control these days," Sabrina says and then giggles.

"Hahah, yeah, don't worry. I took over once he left your supervision. He has been behaving well enough but would always be glad to get some advice from the expert herself."

"Hey, you two! When did you guys become friends? You guys know I'm standing here, right? If I'd known you two would get along so well, I wouldn't have brought him here."

"Don't worry about him. He's been a little angsty lately planning this whole operation. Well, it's nice to finally voice-meet you. We will continue this later. For now, I need to stay on the lookout in case the guard comes back. See you later!" Seven says, leaving the room right after.

"So how are you doing? How is Odin doing as well? You told me last time that he was getting a little tired. I hope he's all better now."

"You know how it is—same old same old. After you left by a bit, it was weird around here, but we were bound to get used to it after a while. I can tell you one thing that hasn't changed though, your voice is still just as funny when it pops up on the system speakers as the day you installed it. It still puts a smile on Odin's face, and that always warms my heart. Since he's been a little off these days, but he's doing well overall. So what's new on your end?"

"Yeah, let's not talk about the voice system. I knew I should have changed it, but now after hearing Odin likes it, I am glad it turned out how it did. Anyway, life here is pretty dull as well. You can already see that it's impossible to come down and visit you guys. It's all done on purpose I'm sure. I do have some major life updates, though! Where do I even start? Remember my watch? It's not only a watch, but it's also a communication device as well, and it has the ability to talk to the people on the outside."

"Wait what? Outside outside? Like the contaminated world outside? So, I am assuming that someone spoke to you? Tell me more!" Sabrina exclaims in a higher pitch than her usual tone.

I tell her all about my interactions and discoveries with the outside world and Zel. Sabrina is amazed but apathetic at the same time. Sabrina later on asks.

"Well, listen, Isim, this is all super interesting, but there is no real proof of people living outside. We can't be too sure of the quality of the air outside either. All I am trying to say here is be careful because there is no turning back if you decide to venture outside."

Always the voice of reason, but it's hard to listen now. I'm too consumed with the idea that my entire world might be a lie. "Don't worry, Sabrina. I am super curious, but I won't be reckless. I will figure out these secrets with a proper plan. What if life outside is just as good as it currently sounds, though? Do you think you'd join me on such an adventure?"

"You know I can't, Isim. I need to be by Odin's side, but I'm envious of those muffins. Listen, you need to figure out a way to sneak some down here."

"I will, I will. Don't worry. We'll figure out a way," I say as I start reminiscing on my time in the lower levels that I took for granted.

We keep chatting and catching up about everything that we couldn't easily communicate through our messages. Not until I notice Seven waving at me from the door, suggesting we should start leaving soon.

"Sabrina, I need to go right now but let's do this more often. Just stick to the time, and it should be fine even to meet every day. Let's try to meet every day for three days just to be on the safe side. What do you say?"

"Great, yeah, that's perfect. Send my regards to Seven as well. Talk to you soon then!"

I unplug the cable and hang the end of it to the secret hook by the edge. I head directly to the door where Seven is and nod to head out. I felt lighter as we started walking back. It was like happiness streaked through me like a comet and sucked all the negative energy I had been hoarding right through me.

Seven looks at me with that same smirk whenever I bring up the topic of Sabrina. "So I didn't get to talk much to Sabrina," I knew it was coming before he even mentioned her name, "But she seems really nice. I see why you guys are close."

I wonder if he's pulling from some plot in his romance books, the only real escape he gets. I smile in response. "She is. I am glad you like her. I do hope one day we can all just chill and relax in person."

Odin seems to be doing well, but a part of me is still worried. I know how he operates. He would never say something is wrong unless it reaches its peak state. He doesn't like to worry us about his 'small issues', trying to keep us at ease. Anyway, I really do hope he is getting better now. I believe in Sabrina's healing powers.

We continue our short chat as we walk back home just to repeat this whole routine again for the next couple of weeks.

Work, eat, chat, and catch up with Sabrina. The few visits Seven starts joining the calls. We get so used to the guard routine, and he never alters from it. Seven, Sabrina, and I grow tighter as time went by. Seven now knows all about the life in the lower levels, including Odin since I keep bringing him up as well.

During that period, I have still been visiting Zel, but the frequency of my visits has been reduced. Seven joined me a few times for those trips, but he isn't as free to do so because of his deadlines.

We have been going with this new routine for a month now. This all changed after that month. At the beginning of the fifth week, I head to the usual meet-up with Sabrina. I connect my walkie-talkie and await her to connect as well. We usually just wait for the other person to say hello first based on who gets there second. This time, however, I never got to hear Sabrina's 'Hello'. I waited for as long as I could before the guard would usually come but to no avail.

I have kept going there every day for that week in case Sabrina ends up showing up. I sit alone, mostly with no responses. I sit there for hours, aimlessly staring at the walls awaiting some sign that everything will be fine. Then, on the eighth day of that week, Sabrina finally shows up.

"Hello." Sabrina's voice seems different the second I hear that 'Hello'. There is a slight quiver in her voice. "Isim, are you there?"

Everything about her tone leaves me unnerved. Something is wrong. Something is very wrong. "Hey, Sabrina, is everything alright? I was so worried. What happened?"

"Sorry, I just got so busy that last week. It's Odin." Her voice gets a little calmer as she spoke. "He has been hiding his symptoms from us. I knew he was having trouble with his health, but he wouldn't let me check him up and kept saying he was alright until last week when he got so tired, and I saw his blood-filled napkins caused by his coughs. Who knows how long he's been hiding this, and he still refuses to admit that something is wrong. It is just a bad cough. It will pass, he keeps saying."

My heart sinks. "Oh. Well, keep me updated, please. Let me know if there's anything that I can do from my end. Maybe I can pass by the pharmacy and sneak you whatever you need. Just please tell me what you would need, and I am ready!"

"Will do, don't worry. The issue right now is figuring out what the cause is. I just can't treat him without knowing what's actually the problem. He is just so stubborn."

We keep on chatting for the next few minutes, but my mind is just stuck looping around Odin. I just worry and feel so helpless. I hate that we can't even give the proper care to the people living in the lower levels. I can't even pass by just to see how Odin is doing or even say hello. I hope I can one day figure out a way to bypass this annoying system and visit the lower levels.

"Well, anyway, Isim, I need to run back to Odin. He gets tired unexpectedly and starts coughing uncontrollably. I see he tries so hard to make it seem normal, but it's mostly out of his control at this point. So I'll talk to you later," Sabrina says. Her voice is soft, almost fragile as if her heart was about to be shattered. But perhaps her heart was already broken.

"It will all get better, Sabrina. You take care of yourself and Odin. We'll talk soon," I say with a heavy heart. I wish I could just give her the hug she deserves right now.

The next few days go by so slowly. I have been brainstorming about ways to bypass the security system on the dumbwaiter. Maybe, this way, I can sneak to the lower levels, even if for just a bit.

The last few days, I have been casually meeting up with Sabrina, but one thing I didn't mention to her was that I was also working on figuring out my way into the security system to activate the dumbwaiters secretly. I just recently finished up my latest creation. I can easily scan any of the guard's access cards and copy all the information onto an empty card of mine. I just need to get close enough to one of the guards for a scan, and we are good to go.

I plan to surprise Sabrina with my visit as well. So in the next few days, we meet as we normally would, except for a couple of missed days between our meetups due to Odin's health. I hope once I make it downstairs, I can even sneak back home to see Odin.

My plan will commence tonight before my usual meet-up with Sabrina. I finish up my daily work routine and head directly to dumbwaiter block. It is 7:05 pm right now, and I notice the guard walking away from his spot. It is time. I walk directly toward the guard pretending to be distracted by the interesting-looking buildings in the area as if I haven't seen everything around here for the millionth time.

The moment we are close enough, I pretend to stumble and fall on the guard as I attempt to scan his ID card at the same time. I drop my bag as well as an extra distraction.

"I am so sorry, sir. This is my first time in this area, so I was just studying the area and didn't see you in front of me. These buildings here are very interesting and different from the other residential areas. Can I help you with anything?"

"Look in front of you next time," the guard says in a very rough tone as he continues his walk.

"Apologies, sir," I cry back to him as he is walking away.

I look down at my scanner, and I see the green light indicator. The scan was successful. A few seconds and the guard is out of sight. I head directly into the building unit. I rush to the dumbwaiter and hook my device to the security panel. Anxious as hell, but it should work. I wish I told Seven to come and keep guard but whatever now.

I connect my walkie-talkie to check if Sabrina is already downstairs. She missed the last visit, so it's been six days now since we last spoke. No response. I will go down in all cases and surprise her and Odin at home. I can't wait to see their faces when I show up.

I climb inside the dumbwaiter and start my descent. The lift belts finally come to a halt. I open the door just to see Sabrina right in front of me. Her face is filled with shock: shock and sorrow. I feel a sharp stabbing pain in my heart and stomach.

I have never seen Sabrina in this way, yet now she is on the brink of bursting into tears. A second later, she can no longer keep holding it. Her hands are shaking as she wipes off her tears. I climb out of the lift, grabbing her closer to me as I wrap my arms around her.

I don't think I am ready to hear what she has to say next, but I ask. "What happened? Is everything alright Sabrina?"

Her bottom lip quivers in response. "It's… It's Odin. He passed away a couple of days ago. I couldn't… I couldn't help him," Sabrina says with tears coming down.

My knees feel weak. I don't know if it's because I am sitting crouched in the lift, or from the news I just have heard, or a combination of both. I hug Sabrina tighter as she leans her head closer to my chest.

"It's not your fault. I know you did your best. Everything is going to be alright; I am here now," I say, trying to calm her down.

We stand there embracing each other in silence for a couple of minutes after that. Felt like an eternity, I wouldn't have minded staying there forever just, so I won't face the reality of the situation. Odin is dead, and I can't even be there in time to say goodbye.

Chapter 7

I have dreamed of being with Sabrina and Odin for the longest time since I left this place. Finally, here I am with both of them again, and it dawns on me how much I've missed home. Seeing the neighborhood again makes me feel like I never left and regret that I did. I wish it was in my power to be around more often. Sabrina is sitting by my side, looking as weary as ever.

I drop off the flowers I got with me at the memorial wall. His name is inscribed on the wall, and it is the latest name added to the wall. Seeing Odin's name on the wall just makes everything feel so real.

We sit there mourning our loss for a while. There are a lot of other flower arrangements and gifts left in honor of Odin. He was loved by all and will be dearly missed. We then head out to our old hangout spot near the river. No one is usually there, so it's a perfect spot to relax and collect our thoughts. No one knows I have sneaked back here except for Sabrina.

"I just wish he told me. Maybe if I had known in time, I could have done something about it. But he just had to be so damn stubborn. I hate this. I feel so lost, Isim. I don't know what I'm supposed to do right now."

"I know, I know Sabrina. It is hard, but we must endure and move forward, and if you ever need anything, I'll always be here for you, and you know it," I say as I grab her closer to me.

Sabrina looks down at a flower she brought with her, fiddling with the white pedals. We sit silently for the next hour or so. It feels comforting just sitting by her side, even in silence. I hate that I can't stay here for too long. I need to head back to the upper levels on the next guard break. It is currently way past midnight, so we should start heading back before people start waking up.

We both wake up past noon, barely having any energy in us after last night. I head to the kitchen and make her some breakfast. Once done, I head to Sabrina's room, where she's been painting.

"Hey, Sabrina, I made you breakfast. You need to eat something. How are you feeling today?"

Her voice is low when she says, "It's alright, and I'm not feeling hungry."

I drop off the plate in front of her on the table near her painting supplies. "Come on, for me? Just take a bite, at least. I made it the way you like it, with a hint of honey drizzled. Just don't accidentally dip your brush in your food," I say with a smirk in an attempt to cheer her up.

I move the plate closer to Sabrina as I pat her shoulder and smile. I have never been the emotional kind of person, but that felt natural as I tried to comfort her. She nods and takes a fragile bite out of the sandwich. I can tell she's forcing it, but it's fine, as long as she eats something.

"I really wish I could stay longer Sabrina, but tonight I need to head back up before anyone starts suspecting I disappeared. I will definitely be coming over more often now, though, since I figured out a way to sneak past the system."

Sabrina nods again and goes back to dipping her brush into the paint for another stroke across the canvas. The next few hours are spent at home distracting ourselves with random chores or activities. I try to make small talk about literally anything, but Sabrina doesn't say much during the whole stay. Once it is time, we say our goodbyes, promising I will visit her again in three days.

The next couple of weeks go by so slowly. I visit Sabrina once a week, staying at her place for the night till the next day. Seven comes sometimes for a quick chat with Sabrina to cheer her up. Seven always has his way with people, so with time, he manages to get to her. It has been a rough couple of weeks, but I like to think that life is getting back to normal bit by bit.

It's been tough on us all, but I try to stay as positive as possible, at least for Sabrina's sake. I have been trying to make conversations with her for weeks, but I just keep getting dead-end responses, and I don't blame her, but it just hurts on the inside seeing her like this. I have started to get worried for her till she finally breaks her silence with a shocking announcement.

"Isim, I have been thinking. I want to leave this place. What was your plan for leaving and meeting up with Zel," Sabrina says with her sad yet hopeful eyes.

For the first time in a very long time, I feel a change in her spirit. I can sense her determination from that statement like she's been thinking about this whole topic for the last few weeks and has finally won the argument in her head to make a move.

"Are you sure this is what you want to do, Sabrina? I will always be here to visit you. You also still have everyone around here to support you if ever needed. You don't need to rush into…" I try to finish my sentence, but Sabrina interrupts me.

"Listen, I have been thinking about this for a while now, and I am not rushing into anything. So let me know if you still want to go out because I want in, and I am convinced of my choice."

I am impressed at Sabrina's determination, but I do hope she does not regret this later on.

"I haven't thought about this plan for a while now, but I did have a rough plan from before. Let me refresh on it and finalize it, and we can reopen the topic at a later stage to discuss it further. This way, I can tell Seven if he's interested, get more information from Zel about this plan, and you have more time to think this through. Don't forget. There is no going back if we are to move forward with this plan. Sound good?"

"Okay, but don't take too long." Sabrina gives me a very faint smile that started fading away slowly but just enough to trigger the widest smile on my face. "Okaay!" I blurt.

Later that night, I start brainstorming ideas on how we can achieve such a stunt with the least amount of risk involved. We still don't know if the outside world really is clean. What if we get caught after we leave, would they let us in or just close the doors on us? And, if we get caught before we leave, would they force us out or put us in jail? A lot of take into consideration, which is why the plan needs to be perfect and accommodate for all scenarios that get thrown our way.

The next morning, I bring Seven up to date with Sabrina's interest. He is very interested, and we start planning it right there and then as if our actual work was just a side job. By the end of our session, we had a fairly finalized plan. Of course, anything is prone to happen generally, but we tried our best to accommodate each scenario as it comes.

The plan right now starts off by gathering the essential resources for such a trip. This includes food, water, a few survival items like a knife, a fire starter, a compass, and so on. I will try to fit everything in a bag later today to make sure our carry-on won't be too heavy but fits all the necessary items required. This is all prone to be altered if needed for the sake of a successful mission.

The next step will be to manage a route and time of the day to sneak in Sabrina from the lower levels without being noticed and wait it out till nighttime. That way, we can avoid being seen or getting caught as an extra precaution. We then gather all our essential belongings and head out to the tunnel, where the most critical step lies in determining our fate.

I will need to play around with the security panel to unlock the door to the outside world without being detected, assuming it is all connected to a central security system. I might as well be able to program it to open the door back for us in case we face any issues in the outside world that would change our minds.

I will work on that security bypass later this week. For now, this sums up the plan for the grand escape. I will need to update Zel about this master plan, though, just for her to be ready if we make it to her.

Later that same night, I head to Zel to check up on her and update her on our current plan, so she can meet us if she really is nearby us on the outside.

"Hey, Zel, you there? Listen I need to tell you of some major updates, and I need you to focus as much as you can, so you can help us out here."

"Hey, Isim! Oooh, that sounds exciting. So tell me, what do you have going on? I am all ears."

Zel hears me out quietly. She usually isn't this quiet for so long. Always up to the next question or thought to discuss until today.

"Well, that is very interesting, and I am so excited to be able to meet you guys finally. I need to warn you, though. If all three of you guys come over, we will need to move stuff around to make space. Otherwise, you guys are most welcome. You guys can even start helping around with the chores around the house. There isn't much work to do, but I do hate doing the dishes, so maybe you guys would take over this task as payment for your stay," Zel says with a chuckle.

Her voice is filled with excitement, and I do look forward to finally meeting her in person. Hopefully, everything goes as planned.

"So tell me more about the area you live in. Since this plan will come to fruition, I would like to gather as much information as possible. Anything will help, really."

"Oh, where do I even start? So you already know about my house. The same cabin I told you about before. It has an attic for storing different tools and other stuff. The inside of the house has the basic rooms and items such as a stove, bed, chairs, etc.

"I have a small garden in the back where I try to grow anything from vegetation that I can come by. My area is surrounded by a lot of grass generally. The house is surrounded by a wall of trees all around but the radius of the wall of trees is fairly long. Long enough to fit maybe two other cabins between the cabin I live in and the wall. I think that sums it up. Did I miss anything?"

"Oh, wow, that's actually very useful information, thanks! It will be hard to spot it in a forest but still easier with this helpful information. Thanks!"

"You know what, I have an idea. I will attach a big yellow cloth to a stick, like a flag, on the house's rooftop, so it makes it easier to spot maybe. That way, it will be much easier to find me."

"That would actually be awesome. So, there is no defined date for the escape, but I will try to keep you posted. It's going to be a busy couple of days here trying to finalize everything. One thing for sure is you will hear from me on the day of the escape. Let's hope everything goes according to plan, and we'll see you soon!"

"I can't wait! Do you think you could get me a muffin as well from there when you come? I would love to try it out since you mentioned previously that it's so delicious."

I chuckle lightly. "Yes, of course! I definitely can fit in one muffin for you. You will love it, I'm sure of it. Okay, listen, I need to go now. I'll keep you updated as we move forward. I'll see you soon!"

"Sounds good. Good luck and goodbye then!" Zel says as I turn off my walkie-talkie and head back home. I have a lot of work to do.

Later that night, I start refining the plan and working on my gadgets. I think I will only have one shot to try to hack into the security panel on the final door. Hopefully, there are no alarms set on the panel. We only have one chance to make everything work and won't need more than that, honestly, since we are leaving anyway.

A week passes by. During that period, Seven and I kept going back and forth between the tunnel and the dumbwaiter building unit. Just to make sure everything went as planned, with no surprise hurdles coming up. Sabrina and Zel are both kept up to date with any developments in the plan. Nothing major changes at this point of the plan.

Two weeks pass. A lot of work and attention has been put into planning this mission. The plan shall commence tonight. Seven is currently on standby outside the dumbwaiter building unit, keeping an eye on the returning guards. I am on the walkie-talkie with Sabrina as she prepares herself to get into the dumbwaiter. A couple of minutes pass, and I see the doors open. Sabrina has arrived.

She emerges with her eyes shining bright in zeal. She stands there for barely a second, and at a moment's notice, we hug instantly in some sort of relief as if the plan had just finished. That short moment we had, felt like the whole world's problems had been brushed off my chest.

Right after that, we head back to Seven. Sabrina notices Seven, and she smiles and waves to him as we all start heading back to our place.

"It's so nice to finally meet you in person Sabrina, you seem just as sweet in person as our walkie-talkie chats," Seven whispers.

We have planned our path in a way to avoid people as much as we could. Always on the lookout throughout the walk, and if seen, we have a plan B for such a scenario. Seven seems stress-free throughout the walk, relaxing me too. For a moment, I think back to the first time I met. How he so easily made me feel welcome, not isolated, and hasn't missed a moment to comfort me since that day.

I make a mental note to thank him for his friendship later when all this is over.

The moment we reach and enter my place, everyone sighs in relief. I turn my back for an instant to close the door, and the next second, I hear a loud yet soft thump behind me. I see Sabrina lying down on the couch.

"So this whole place is yours, huh, you guys are living such a lavish life here. Do you also have one of those cars or bikes I saw outside?" Sabrina asks in a sarcastic tone.

"No, I don't, but not that it matters anyway, we will be leaving all of this soon if everything goes according to plan," I say as I see Sabrina's smirk fade into a blank expression.

Seven heads out to prepare his stuff for the trip. He will also update Zel on the plan one last time before we officially head out. I leave Sabrina to relax for a bit till it's time to leave at night. I am ready for the most part, but I must double-check everything is in order for our trip. We head out at 1:00 am exactly. Seven will follow us right after just, so it doesn't look suspicious in case anyone notices us all grouped up on a mission.

Sabrina and I relax for a bit till the time comes. She seems in a much better state compared to the last time we met, relaxed and at ease. I double-check everything since there is still some time to waste till we head out. Sabrina suddenly stands up in determination.

"Is there a way we can chill outside? I feel like I'm suffocating in here," Sabrina says with a weary expression.

"You know what, I think I have the perfect spot where we can relax till it's time. Follow me." It's a new spot I discovered recently. No one usually goes on the rooftops of the houses here, and I found a way there that no one utilizes. So I think it would be a perfect spot to relax for a bit before our big move.

We head up and lie down on a mini blanket I got with me. This way, no one can spot us, and we get to relax outdoors for a bit. We just lay there for a short while, taking in the calmness of the place until Sabrina breaks the silence.

"I miss Odin. I really thought I could push through as time went by, but it does not get any easier Isim. It all just sucks. I miss him so dearly. I used to still pass by his room in case he needed anything and then realized he was no longer with us. What makes it worse is that you moved up as well too. The house is way too quiet, and I hate it. People used to visit at first, but then everyone went back to their usual daily routine. Right now, I am just so glad I got to see you again."

"I am sorry you had to go through all of this on your own. I really wish I could have been with you when this all went down. I am not going anywhere now though." Sabrina gives me a warm half-smile.

We lie down in silence after that for a little while till Sabrina breaks the silence again.

"So do you really think your father is out there? I really hope we find him, but what if it turns out he is not outside?

We might not have another chance to come back inside the bunker."

"I've thought about this a million times, and I know what I am risking here, but I think it's still worth a shot. I know I will regret it, and it will keep bugging me for however long I stay in here, so I need to go and see for myself. Life outside might turn out to be better than expected after all. Who knows…?"

Sabrina nods in agreement. As she is about to ask another question, my alarm goes off. It is time.

"Sorry to interrupt. We'll have to continue our chat later on once we can breathe the fresh air. We need to stick to the schedule. Are you ready?" Sabrina nods, and we both head down, preparing ourselves to leave.

We start our walk to the tunnel. The streets are empty. Nothing but silence ensues in the city. Sabrina is keeping her head low, trying to avoid eye contact with any potential bypassers. Throughout the walk, we kept silent except for a few 'this way' and directional nods.

It was weird because I have gone through this path so many times, and no one really cared. I used to sing to myself at times or walk while kicking a can with me as I moved forward. This time though, I felt so much pressure from even being seen.

We finally reach the alley, and as we walk through the surrounding junk, I feel a presence around us. Before going in, I take a quick look, but no one is around. We then just continued our walk forward into the tunnel.

"Is everything alright? Are we expecting someone right now?" Sabrina asks with a semi-anxious tone.

"No, it's alright. I thought I heard someone, but I might be just nervous right now. Anyway, it doesn't really matter. Let's keep moving. There is no looking back right now, pun intended," I say anxiously as I try to keep Sabrina calm. Sabrina gives me half a smile as we keep moving forward.

I notice Sabrina's fascination with the tunnel while we walk through, reminding me of the first time I walked here. Finally, we reach the door that leads to the suits. We enter and suit up while waiting for Seven. He is supposed to reach right after us in fifteen minutes.

While waiting, Sabrina observes the outside world from the window. I try to keep an eye out on the other door awaiting Seven's arrival. A couple of minutes in, I see some movement through the tunnel. Seven has finally made it, and he looks ecstatic.

Seven opens the door. "Are you guys ready to…" Seven says as he gets interrupted by a sudden haul.

A dark figure emerges from the dark. He has a hold of Seven's bag as he tries to drag him backward from our room. Seven acts fast and takes off his bag in an attempt to run forward without his bag toward us. The mysterious person's reaction was instant. The dark figure switches and grabs Seven's shirt collar forthwith.

"GO GUYS, GOOO! I'LL JOIN YOU GUYS LATER! TAKE IT FAST AND GO!" Seven says as he steps backward, ramming into the person and simultaneously throwing the backpack through the door. "CLOSE THE DOOR!"

As much as it pains me to do it, I listen to Seven and take the bag and close the door. We have to keep moving forward with the plan, sadly without Seven.

The mysterious figure finally shows himself strangling Seven. Seven tries to free himself but struggles to unclench himself from his tight grip. It's the same guard from the dumbwaiter.

"I might finally get out of this dreadful job once I deliver you guys to the higher-ups. OPEN THE DOOR NOW!" the guard says as he struggles to open the door while holding onto Seven.

"You guys really think you can leave and survive outside alone, YOU WON'T STAND A CHANCE. You won't survive a day out there, so OPEN UP THESE DOORS!" The guard starts running out of patience as he attempts to shake the door uncontrollably.

I have planned for every scenario, but I did not expect this to happen. How could I have expected him to have been following us and capture Seven on top of it all? I move Sabrina forward to the door; we must keep going. I open up the outside doors. I can hear a surge of fresh outside air coming through the door slits as the doors open. Finally, we are one step away from being free from this bunker.

"We will come back and get you back, Seven! Just stay strong and be patient!" I scream to Seven as I wave back to him. Seven sees us and nods toward the outside door to move forward.

Sabrina and I both take our first steps together into the outside world.

Chapter 8

The whole world around us is covered with darkness yet somehow in a continuous fight with the luminescence coming from the moon. The only source of brightness in this dark world. We've lived our entire lives under artificial lights, and our nights were never really as dark as it is now.

Have we really made the right choices? We both pondered, standing outside, not that any of it mattered right now. Sabrina taps my left shoulder, looks at me with a slight asymmetric smile on her face, deep sadness pasted over the top of it all, and nods to move forward.

I take one last quick glance at what used to be our home for all our lives. The structure is very basic from the outside. A worn-out dome with the final door that led to our freedom attached to it. The bunker was abandoned for years, so you could see the weathered concrete walls with small cracks here and there.

The paint on it is peeling off as expected yet the peculiar thing is what is written on the side of the dome. The letters are a little worn out, but you can read what is written on it. 'Pill 0'. Nothing else. Doesn't matter now anyway.

I turn back to Sabrina, and we start our walk into the world. To our new and hopeful start. Even though we know

Zel is outside, we are not confident enough to remove our helmets until we see her. We still need to keep in mind that different zones might have different levels of air pollution. So until we meet up with Zel, we can get more confident in removing our suits.

We are walking around but at a very slow pace, and my eyes keep bouncing back and forth between the world around us and the oxygen meters. We need not exhaust ourselves too much and not waste unnecessary energy and oxygen until we reach our destination.

Our silent walk was soon interrupted by some rumbling in the bushes nearby us. I look around but can't see anything yet. I see Sabrina's facial expressions, and she's trying to act brave, but her eyes tell a different story. Suddenly a cracking sound is heard from behind the tree right beside the bush. Sabrina's facial expressions finally give in and join her fearful eyes.

She moves closer to me and grabs my hand. A weird-looking creature emerges. I have read about many wild animals and creatures, but this… thing does not bear any resemblance to anything I have ever seen or read about. The creature stands on all four of its legs with its front two legs built like a mantis, razor-sharp edges ready to attack.

We all stand there transfixed by the terror of the situation. Those rumors Seven mentioned previously were all true. What is more terrifying is that the creature's head mostly consists of ferociously looking teeth going across the front half of its head.

My jaw tightens, and my entire body grows stiff. I'm afraid to breathe, but I whisper to Sabrina through our suit's communication system. "On my mark, we run as fast as we can in the opposite direction, okay?" Sabrina acknowledges me without making any sound or movement. "Ready? GO!"

We both don't even look back and halt out of there for our lives as fast as we possibly can. I have a grip on her hand as we run forward through the trees and bushes. My heart is racing, and we can hear each other's uncontrollable breathing as we run through the woods. I take a glimpse backward, and I no longer see the creature and start to relax for a second. A few more seconds later, a similar-looking creature appears out of nowhere, right in front of us. This time it is accompanied by two other ones.

"SHIT SHIT, GO RIGHT, GO RIGHT!"

Just as we are running, we reach a dead-end. We are forced to run through the bushes, but little did we know that just twenty meters into those bushes was a small cliff. One step was on solid ground and the very next into thin air. We took that step downward without even realizing it until it was too late. Gravity feels like it has doubled on our already exhausted and adrenaline-filled bodies.

It is inevitable. We start rolling and getting slammed into whatever rocks lie in our plummet back to the bottom of the pit. I see my backpack ripped from my back, rolling away from us till we both finally hit and smash into the bottom of the hill. Darkness ensues my world as I lose consciousness.

***

A ray of light sneaks its way right between the cracks of the trees around us and right into my right eye. My body feels numb like I haven't used it in a week. I can barely sit, but I arch forward and look at my watch just to realize that it's only been four hours. I glimpse by the edge of my eye a foot with large shoes. It's Sabrina! She's still unconscious lying near me.

Our suits are badly damaged, but if it wasn't for the ruggedness of the suits, we could have been in a much worse state than we currently are in. My helmet has a small crack but seems still functional. Right beside Sabrina lies my walkie-talkie broken in half and damaged from the fall. We are all alone right now.

I grab Sabrina and shake her shoulder lightly. "Sabrina, Sabrina! Are you okay? Wake up, Sabrina." Her suit doesn't seem to have taken much damage; in fact, her helmet doesn't seem like it even left the bunker aside from it being extra dusty from the fall.

Sabrina finally opens up her eyes, slowly realizing what just happened.

"Are you alright, are you hurt anywhere? Let me help you up. Try standing up with me."

I lift her up, and everything seems to be fine. "Thank God! You're alright. That was a nasty fall, but we still need to be careful. We still don't know where those creatures are and if there's even more of them."

Sabrina shakes her head calmly as she looks down at my chest, where my oxygen meter lies on the suit. She then switches immediately to look at the meter on her chest and back at me with fright in her eyes.

"Isim, your suit is damaged! How long have we been out for? You're almost out of oxygen."

"Dammit, we really don't need this right now. We need to start moving really quickly and find the cabin before the monsters find us first. I think I have a few minutes left till I run out of oxygen," I say as I pause for a few seconds collecting my thoughts to form a proper plan.

Every breath matters right now, and I need to be as efficient as possible. Just as I am about to reveal my master plan, Sabrina's eye brightens up. It's those eyes again. I don't like the looks she's giving me.

"Isim. Behind you. They're back. They got more of their friends as well," Sabrina whispers to me slowly.

I don't even look back not to cause any sudden movement until needed. I can feel my heartbeat pounding out of my heart like thunder striking.

"Listen to me. There is no way I will make it out with my oxygen levels. So you run, and I will distract them. Okay!" I say as Sabrina's eyes start getting watery.

"No, no, no, no, no, no. You can't. No, don't," Sabrina says, shaking her head profusely.

"Sabrina, please go!" I prepare myself mentally just before I turn around, but I need to make sure Sabrina actually does start running.

Sabrina finally gives up and runs. It is my turn now; I turn around and instantly start shaking my hands around as a distraction. Only to realize that there are no creatures whatsoever around us. Did they run away already? What happened? I need to head back to Sabrina before she goes too far.

I start screaming, "SABRINAAA! SABRINA! COME BACK. THE MONSTERS LEFT US."

Sabrina hears me, and I see her slowing down her pace, still breathing heavily. Then, just as she turns back around to face me, her eyes get reignited with those same fearful eyes. It can't be. I am an idiot! Why did I have to scream?

This time I look back instantly to see how close they are to me. To my disbelief, I see nothing again. Sabrina's eyes are still locked on those 'monsters'. Something is wrong here. It suddenly dawned upon me. It can't be. There is no way it is what I'm thinking.

"Sabrina, stay where you are. They won't attack you if you don't move. I have a plan," I whisper in a soft voice as I try to get closer to her.

I grab hold of Sabrina by her shoulders. "You trust me, right? I need you to close your eyes. Please, I promise you everything will be alright."

Her eyes are shut now, and I can feel her whole body shaking out of fear. It doesn't take me much time, but I can feel her heartbeat bursting out of her chest as she trembles at what's about to happen next.

"Sabrina. Try to focus on me, open your eyes slowly, and keep focusing on me. Okay."

A single tear slides right between the corner of her eyelids as she opens her eyes, staring right into my eyes. She can see me as clear as day with nothing protecting my head from fall damage anymore.

"Don't worry, I got you. Everything will be all right," I say gently, placing my hands on the edges of her helmet where the release button lies. I swiftly remove her helmet from her head, keeping eye contact accompanied by a light smile.

"What do you think of the fresh air? It's nice, isn't it?"

Sabrina takes a short but deep breath in and closes her eyes just for a second. She can't help but feel relaxed just for that second as she almost forgets about everything going on around us. Right after, her eyes open up again, she takes a glimpse behind me and realizes that the creatures are gone. I can tell she is relieved but still anxious since they could still come back.

"How did you do this? What happened? Where did those monsters go? How are you able to breathe freely? How am I able to breathe freely? What the hell is happening!" Sabrina exclaims in relief but with a confused, anxious half-smile.

"The adrenaline rush was getting the best of us, but while running for what could have been my last breath, I realized something. Right at the edge of my helmet was a crack big enough to poke a finger right through. That's when I realized that I was actually breathing the fresh air from outside this whole time. Since I was running out of oxygen anyway, I might as well risk it and remove my helmet altogether."

"That doesn't explain how you got rid of the monsters, though?" Sabrina exclaims in a quiet voice so as to not alert the monsters in case they were still nearby.

"Well, that's the best part. Seems like these helmets were actually equipped with virtual reality technology. I read about that a very long time ago but didn't think it was real. All the creatures felt very real, but in reality, they were all holograms built right in front of our eyes from the screens of our helmets! In fact, put your helmet back on and see for yourself!" So I say with confidence but also still inconspicuously afraid of the possibility that my theory is incorrect.

Sabrina puts her helmet back on, and a minute later, the monsters are back.

"Oh my God! You're a genius. We could have suffocated in our suits from our fear of these creatures and the toxic air. You're amazing Isim! What would I have ever done without you?" Sabrina says with each word coming out of her barely grasping for air as she hugs me tightly with all the energy she has left after everything we have gone through.

We both start to take off our useless suits. We relax for a bit on two specific rocks that looked like the most comfortable rock chairs. Smooth like a pebble and big enough to fit a person. As if those rocks have been waiting for this exact moment in time for us to stop here and sit on them.

We both sit in silence, staring at the sky that seems even more blue and beautiful than it ever was in the helmet or in books. Sabrina releases a loud sigh as she leans her head on my shoulder. Leaves fell around us from different gusts of winds that would pass by and hit our sweaty faces to give us a much-needed cool-off from all the running we had to go through. I would stay here forever if it was up to me, but we need to keep moving.

We embrace this moment of silence, for it was much needed after today. I couldn't tell how long we sat there, but I felt my muscles unclench and become almost jelly-like. I look down and see Sabrina form a light smile on her face as if we just solved world hunger.

"This is a really nice, Sabrina." My thoughts are phased for just a second by the crunches of leaves and twigs around us. "But we should really start moving now. The cabin must be close after all this running. I can feel it."

We start our walk into the unknown with so much confidence and relief. I don't think anything will unnerve us after our last experience. We keep walking for a few minutes till, finally, the trees stop getting as crowded right in front of us. As we move forward, the image gets clearer. It is just as she described it, right in front of us.

Between a crowd of trees, we see a clear area. The cabin is right in the middle of that crowd. One thing is different, however. The grass is so long all around the cabin, and there are no plants or any hints of a garden, as Zel described. The yellow flag is nowhere to be seen either. Is this the spot? This must be it. The formation of the trees is identical to the description Zel gave us. Zel probably just forgot to place the flag. This has to be it. Right?

Chapter 9

A quick look at the cabin and a sensation of familiarity follows, especially with how Zel has been describing the cabin in our talks. Yet, at the same time, everything looks so worn out and different. We keep moving forward toward the cabin. It kind of feels nice walking through the thick grass.

I can feel the grass brushing my ankles with every step taken on the soft ground, yet the moment we get closer, we sense a change of terrain hardness under our steps. The ground around the cabin feels a little bit mushier than the rest of the area. I can tell something used to grow in this area around the cabin, just as Zel described it.

We finally reach a halt, Sabrina standing right behind me, waiting for me to make the next move. I am a little nervous about opening the door. However, beyond this door is the main reason we got to where we are now. The doorknob creaks slightly as I twist the handle. I sneak my head through for a peek.

"Hello? Zel? Are you here?" I say looking around for any hint of life as my hopeful words disappear into thin air.

Sabrina stands silently behind me, she tries to look inside between the cracks. Light streaks fill the room from all the gaps between the wooden walls. Dust fills the air just from the simple movement of the door, and you can see it all through the light beams. The room is half-lit simply from all the natural light that is coming into the cabin.

My eyes instantly fall on the messy desk resting in the far corner of the room. It is filled with notebooks and papers that haven't been used for years, it seems, based on the dust in the place. Right beside the desk lies a cylindrical-looking fridge or storage unit covered in dust. There is a small coffee table in the center of the room accompanied by a long couch. There are a couple of mugs with dried-out stains on the edges of the cup on that same table.

You can tell that everything in the room is well-preserved and filled with webs and dust at the same time. I have no idea how long this place has been abandoned for. Still, there doesn't seem to be any interference of any form by animals or outside creatures. Well, aside from those pesky spiders.

I am sure that if any animal was here, they would trip on some of the wires lying around here or at least knock down some of the random household items. Like the coat rack stand or ruin the curtains all around the room. Sabrina and I split around the room to look around for any clue. Anything that could give us information on who was here or what happened.

There is a staircase right beside the fireplace on the far-right side of the room. I am tempted to start upstairs first but that desk with the paper cluster mess feels more enticing to check out since it might reveal more information on who was here last.

I walk toward the desk to notice a photograph. A family of three, it seems. My memory is a bit hazy, but I believe that the person in the center is actually my father. It has been so long since I saw him. Nevertheless, just looking at this image gives off a very refreshing nostalgic feeling.

My father looks just like how I remember him last. Smiling as he carries, who I can only assume is me by his arms and his other hand resting on another older kid's shoulder. I flip the card, and there is a short message written on the back. "Always on my mind, Isim & Duman."

"Isim! Helloooo? Isim, everything alright?" Sabrina calls for me as she walks toward me from the box she was rummaging through. I must have dazed off for a good minute there.

"Yes, yes, all good." I shake it off and raise the picture closer to Sabrina.

"Check this out though. I think I found a picture of my father and me. He was here!"

"Oh, wow, no way. So this could confirm that this cabin is really Zel's place, right?" Sabrina says as she takes a proper glance at the picture.

"Wait, though, who's this other person next to your father? He kind of looks like you, Isim," Sabrina says as she grabs the image and holds it up, side by side with my face. She squints, as she's looking at the picture and me, and a second later, her eyes light up.

"You have a brother! Please tell me you knew you had a brother?"

I nod, but she sees right through my lies. I can't fully recall having a brother, but the idea of a brother feels like a familiar feeling that's long lost.

"Listen, I don't remember; I was too young to remember much. After all, I have been abandoned in the bunker with you guys. So how could I have known, especially with your super cryptic father who won't tell me much about my past. Plus, isn't no one supposed to have more than one kid? But, if so, then this would mean I'm an illegal child. Damn, this changes everything."

Sabrina rolls her eyes at my 'cryptic' comment but then giggles since none of this matters anymore after we left that bunker life behind now. Sabrina nods toward the stairs trying to change the topic as I was starting to go through the random notes and papers on the desk. It is all primarily notes and sketches of some technology that my father was working on that I don't fully understand yet.

"Come on, Isim, let's go upstairs. I am pretty sure we'll find more interesting stuff there," Sabrina says as she leads the way toward the stairs. I sigh and follow her.

The first floor is a bedroom attic with a small window to the greenery outside. There is a bookcase on the side filled with notebooks, which include scientific books about medical diseases, mechanical engineering, and programming. The shelves of the bookcase look like they are overflowing, books are lying all around the bookcase on the ground and around the boxes near it. These boxes are also filled with all sorts of things, from books and notebooks to different computer parts. Each of us takes a box and starts rummaging through.

While rummaging, I take a quick glance around the room. One box in particular near the bed grabs my attention. That box has the initials 'Z.A.' written on it. This has to be one of my father's more personal belongings. I leave the current box I was working to Sabrina and walk toward my new box, carrying the box onto the bed and getting comfortable to start my exploration.

I find a couple of work notes and pencils on top but nothing too important. I look up for a moment to check up on Sabrina's progress. I can see Sabrina across the room diving right in, looking for any clues starting with the bookcase and moving quickly to the boxes nearby.

I see her scrabbling around in the box just to find a bunch of notebooks until she pauses and looks at me with a wide smirk. She raises her hand from the box holding a worn-out teddy bear.

"Look at this cute bear. I feel we saw this somewhere before, right? Oh, wait, I remember actually, you had this in your hand in that picture with your dad!"

"I think you're right, but I have no memory of it when I was young at all. I don't know." A sense of emptiness fills me before Sabrina interrupts it with a snarky comment.

"You used to be so cute with your teddy bear and all. What happened?" Sabrina says with the widest smirk on her face.

"I am starting to have second thoughts on bringing you with me." I tease back rolling my eyes with a mini uncontrollable grin, when in reality I cherish these witty moments we have.

We both get back to work. As I am looking through my box, I notice at the very bottom a very well-preserved leather notebook. Everything is a little bit dusty in the box, but this notebook in particular caught my eye. Its cover is all worn out. Dark brown exterior and is smooth to the touch, even with the scratches all over the cover.

The pages inside are lightly yellowed with age and filled with handwritten notes. I flick the notebook open, skimming through it, and I quickly realize it's a diary. It's my dad's diary. My eyes widen in awe.

Everything else in the box feels irrelevant right now. I grab it and place it on the edge of the bed by itself. The room feels empty. I just head to the window for a quick breather as Sabrina finishes her search through her boxes.

As I gaze through the window, I feel the world is at peace somehow. The breeze flows through the leaves of the trees, with birds chirping nearby. It feels like the moment we got here; serenity ensued the world and leaked through into the cabin as well. This moment right now, after leaving my old life and moving into the new one, is the moment I want to cherish the most. Just serenity. Especially, since that book might be the key to figuring out everything I've always wanted to know about my life.

My thoughts are suddenly interrupted by taps on my shoulder. Sabrina nods to the stairs with a wistful smile. It seems like she is done with her share of looting around for now.

"Isim, want to go downstairs? Relax for a bit. It's been a long day," Sabrina says followed with a sigh.

"Yeah. Let's go, it's been a long day. We definitely deserve it," I say as I grab the diary on my way to the stairs.

We head down. As I am about to sit down by the desk, an image falls off from between the diary pages. It is an old image of who I believe is my father at a much younger age accompanied by a female figure, which I can only assume, is his mother from how similar they look. I flip the image to its back and notice something written at the bottom of the paper, a message in delicate handwriting.

"I will never forget you Zeki, no disease will ever take that away from me. Love, Zel."

I place the diary on the desk right in front of me. I am a little nervous to see what other secrets lie ahead. This can't be a coincidence. Is Zel really my grandma? How did Zel not tell me that that's her son who has been with her this whole time or that she's my grandmother? None of this makes sense right now.

Sabrina by then is already lying down on the couch with a folder she took with her from upstairs. She is casually reading through it like a newspaper. I, on the other side of the room, am sitting in silence trying to clear my mind, so I can start with my diary. I flip open the first page of the diary.

September 3, 2121

Dear Diary,

Days here pass by so slowly. I am not sure what I am doing anymore. I keep getting closer to figuring out the right algorithm to use, but it is never enough. I am not sure how diaries work, yet here I am writing whatever comes to mind. Zel keeps advising me to let thoughts out and discuss them with friends, but I cannot tell her.

Today Zel was struggling with some of her plants not sprouting. That was a tricky fix, but I managed to pull through. I programmed it to grow over the next couple of days for her so that it looked natural. After her plants started growing, I could tell she became a lot happier. Her happiness keeps me going forward to finish my mission, but I do not know for how long I can keep doing this.

I kept reading through more sections like these. They are short but mostly all describe his struggle with his project. Some things don't fully make sense, but I can somehow make sense of it all as I read through. The things mentioned in the diary are mostly describing his day with Zel and his work struggles. A never-ending loop.

I start looking through the notes on the desk, and there lies one especially neat-looking note. It's directed to me. I suddenly feel my heart beat harder once I saw my name.

Dear Isim,

I have no idea if you will ever read or see this note, but I needed to let you know regardless. I never planned for all of this to happen. We live in a cruel world, and I tried my best to keep you and your brother shaded from it all. I am sorry.

After your mother passed away, I was lost. Your grandmother was around to care for you, but you might not remember since you were too young. A few years have passed after your birth, and your grandmother started developing memory loss symptoms.

On top of that, the government started cracking down on the newborn laws. It was a tough time, but I figured that that was the best way to deal with this situation. Odin is my childhood friend, and I trusted him with my life to keep you safe. I moved here to the cabin to take care of your grandmother, who later on fell very ill, and I had to help her. That is where I thought I would utilize my years of research into artificial intelligence.

Maybe I could figure out a way to move her consciousness to a computer system before her Alzheimer's symptoms got the best of her. I cared for her for years through the system and the cryopod here. Still, her heart health deteriorated until it suddenly failed. Part of her mind still

lies in the system connected to the cryopod. She still thinks she is living her normal life here, but in reality, a replica of her mind lives right here in the cryopod system.
This is a lot of take-in, I know. I am sorry for leaving you. I am sorry for laying all of this on you. I am sorry for everything, Isim.

Love,
Zeki

This is all starting to make sense now. So many secrets. Did Odin even know about this? I still have no idea what happened to my father even with all this new information. It feels like I keep going in circles.

As I am staring into the piles of papers and notes on the desk in despair, I notice another note directed to me that I somehow missed. This note is hidden among all the papers on the desk, with the first line of the note peeking through the papers, as if it's calling for me between the crowd.

Dear Isim,
I think this has turned into a habit now. Who knows, maybe one day you will end up reading my messages. Maybe these messages will be read by some random stranger and end there. Nothing is guaranteed, but I would like to think that I am writing to you right now. And especially since this might be my last message.
I think my time here is starting to reach an end, my health started to deteriorate. I got injured on one of my scavenging missions outside, and my wound got really

infected. I am not young anymore. I am afraid that I won't be able to ever see you again. So this is my goodbye.

Even though I had to go my own way away from you and Duman, at least I know for sure that you are both safe. I wish I fought for you harder. I know Odin would do his best, but I really am sorry, and leaving you is my biggest regret. I really am sorry. I just hope you are doing well. I am proud of you no matter what.

I am sure your grandmother would be, too. If you make it here, go visit her in her resting place. She is right beside the lake nearby. That used to be her favorite spot to relax. She will love it if you do. Take care Isim.

Love,
Zeki

I put the note down and realize that right beside the desk is the cryopod mentioned earlier. I couldn't tell what it was when I first entered. It turns out the cylindrical compartment is the cryopod my father mentioned in his note. I clean off the surface of the pod.

The top part of the pod is a see-through section where the patient's body would be placed. It is currently empty, but it seems like the device is still operational. I call for Sabrina and hand her the notes my father left. She reads through them as I start inspecting the cryopod.

"Sabrina, look here. I think this is where the real Zel used to be, and I believe that the Zel we used to talk to is still here. If I can figure out how to operate this technology, we could maybe talk to Zel again and…" I say as Sabrina interrupts me.

Sabrina's eyes narrowed. "Wait, I'm confused. What do you mean? Isn't she dead? At least that's what your father said?" Sabrina says in disbelief.

"I think my father managed to transfer Zel's consciousness into a machine—at least a good part of it. I need to go through all these papers and notes. I am sure some of these schematics will guide me into understanding the full picture of this technology."

"No way! Is this even possible? I kinda knew that there was some sort of snazzy approach to this whole thing but, this! This is next level and so cool. I guess we know where you got your brains from."

I smile back at Sabrina, and with my new exciting objective, start researching how this whole tech could work. Sabrina goes to grab her bag and starts unpacking some of her stuff. I grab whatever I can find from the notes and instructions on the desk and head to the couch to lie down for a bit as I work. As I am reading through some of these cryopod schematics, I realize that we are both starting to get comfortable here as if we are finally home. It might as well be our new home now.

Around an hour pass by. I now have a very basic understanding of this technology, at least just enough to be able to communicate with Zel. Thankfully I managed to grab the damaged walkie-talkie before we left that hill. It is badly damaged, but I think I can fix it just enough to connect it to the system and speak to Zel.

I notice that Sabrina has gone to sleep on the couch. She's definitely exhausted after everything that's happened today, and I don't blame her. In fact, so am I, but my mind won't let me rest right now. Especially after going through all of my father's notes and stuff.

I start tinkering with the walkie-talkie and try to connect it to the cryopod system. The wireless receiver in the walkie-talkie is badly damaged, so I will have to use a wired connection. After a short while, I manage to connect the walkie-talkie to the system. I try to play with the settings of the cryopod system to start it up. I plug in the walkie-talkie.

"Hello? Zel? Can you hear me?"

I get no response. I am 99% sure that this should work, but sadly nothing. I switch to each channel and repeat calling out for Zel. No response whatsoever, not even the static, which makes it even more frustrating. Just as I am about to toss it down and give up, I realize the volume knob was set to zero. I feel so silly. I smile through it and turn it up. Lo and behold, I can hear Zel calling for me.

"Isim! I can hear you. Can you hear me?"

"I hear you! Isim!" Zel says in frustration.

"There you go! I can finally hear you. Sorry, sorry, the volume was set on mute for some reason, and I didn't realize it till now. Have you been speaking for long?"

"Ah, that's alright. It was odd because I could hear you clearly, but you would just ignore me, now it makes sense. I am glad you are back. You disappeared for a while. I thought that was it. You disappeared just like Zeki. I was afraid something had happened. Where are you, though? Did you manage to escape?"

"Sorry, it's a long story. The plan got complicated, and I actually broke my walkie-talkie but just managed to connect it through now."

"Awesome, so where are you now then? Did you find the cabin? I am so excited to meet you guys!"

I pause for a second to collect my thoughts.

"About that. So we did manage to escape, but it turns out we are not in the same area."

I couldn't tell her the full truth. Technically I didn't lie to her, but I don't want to destroy her current reality. Maybe later when the time is right.

"Well, as long as you guys are doing well. That's all that matters at this point. And now that you managed to connect through as well, then it is all good, no worries."

We chat for a short while until Sabrina wakes up from her slumber. Sabrina joins in on our chat a little bit after she wakes up. I made sure before she joined our conversation to update her on the white lie secret, and she agreed it's for the best right now.

We keep on chatting and catching Zel up on our adventure till now. I can see Sabrina describing these monsters and exaggerating some parts of our adventure in a fun way. It is finally good to see her relaxed like this. It hasn't actually been so long since we left the bunker but feels like an eternity with everything that we've gone through.

While chatting I think back to the images I found earlier. I remember Duman, my long-lost brother. Zel might have an idea of where he is or something.

"Zel, I have a random question. You might not know much, but I still must get it off my chest. Do you by any chance know anything about someone called Duman." My heart is beating harder even though I doubt she'd know anything.

"Mmmh. The name feels familiar, but I am sorry Isim, I don't really know. I don't know why the name sounds familiar even," Zel says and pauses for a second to think about it.

"It's alright, didn't really expect you to know, but I had to try and ask since apparently he's my long-lost brother," I say back in disappointment.

"Wait, wait actually. I do recall something now that you mentioned Zeki. So I heard Zeki murmur that name before. He was talking to himself though; he did that sometimes. Mumbling things to himself, but I never questioned him about it since I felt he didn't want to talk about it. He kept saying Duman, pill three or four. That is all I could catch. I'm sorry if that's not so useful," Zel responds.

Sabrina and I both look at each other with puzzled faces, until it hits me. We see the word pill on the outside part of the bunker. Pill 0. Sabrina may have been a little distressed at the time to realize it, but I am sure of it. This can mean that there are more than one bunker or pill. We may have been living in the first pill built.

We briefly discuss these ideas but since we have no concrete evidence of any of them, yet the conversation dies out quickly. The only thought I have right now is that maybe we could try to find these other pills and Duman. I can't help but feel a sense of anticipation building inside me as I thought about meeting Duman, the only family I might have left.

As I dive into my own thoughts, I realize Sabrina has gotten a little quiet. Seconds later, Sabrina's eyes start sparkling with what I could only describe as excitement. It is as if she has discovered the best, most fun thought to share. And I am right. Sabrina asks Zel her question.

"Okay, Zel, question. I know there isn't much to do around but what is your favorite spot around here?"

"Oh, that's an easy one. If you keep walking straight from the backdoor into the forest, you will reach a small lake—my absolute favorite spot. I just sit there staring at the beauty of nature. Sometimes you can spot frogs sitting patiently trying to catch the next meal. The moment he finds his target, you can see it lock its eye till the time is right, and SNAP. Happily munching away."

"Oh, there is a lake here ehm I mean there. Well, that sounds like an interesting spot," Sabrina responds to Zel and looks at me and smirks.

We continue chatting for a little while till Zel excuses herself. It's ironic how she has plans and a schedule in her own world where she technically controls everything.

Right when we disconnect, Sabrina jumps up.

"Isim! Let's go! You heard her. There is a lake nearby. We deserve a break and check it out."

I agree. It has been a long day, and relaxing by the lake does feel like a sound idea. So I grab my bag, and we head there. This place might just be a spot created in her mind and not a real place, but what do we have to lose?

We walk for a short while until the soil under our footsteps turns mushy. We look forward and realize that it is true. The world in her mind is just based on the reality of this place. Trees surround the whole lake except for one small spot. Seems like that is the spot Zel used to sit.

As we get closer, we notice a flat rock standing on the ground near the spot. There is writing on the rock. "In loving memory of Zel 2044-2121."

There is a boulder near the tombstone. Sabrina and I both share it and sit down for a bit. Sabrina turns around and reaches for my backpack. She moves her hand around till she finds what she needs. I wasn't focused on what she grabbed until I noticed it was a muffin split in half on a piece of cloth on her lap. Sabrina bumps her shoulder onto mine.

"I think this is the perfect time to share a muffin. I managed to sneak this one from before and wanted to keep it a surprise. Seven helped me to get it, though, so I have to give him half the credit here," Sabrina says, dressed in the warmest smile I have seen on her.

I close my eyes, feeling like the entire world is at peace. The insects chirp around us; the frogs croak; water ripples with fish. I can't get over the serenity of it all—nature feels soothing. Sabrina then points at one of the frogs nearby, focusing on its target. Eyes locked on its prey and suddenly SNAP.